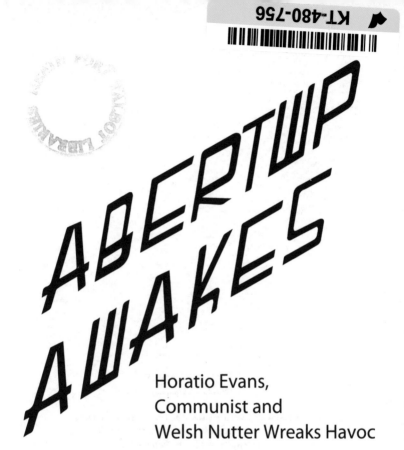

ABERTWP AWAKES

Horatio Evans,
Communist and
Welsh Nutter Wreaks Havoc

Ray Noyes

Cover design: Y Lolfa
Cover picture / illustration: Andy Robert Davies

ISBN: 978 1 78461 170 5

Published and printed in Wales
on paper from well-maintained forests by
Y Lolfa Cyf., Talybont, Ceredigion SY24 5HE
e-mail ylolfa@ylolfa.com
website www.ylolfa.com
tel 01970 832 304
fax 832 782

A Hero is born in a 1,000;
Wise men are revealed in 10,000;
Fools are everywhere.

After Plato

Preface

I N CASE THE reader infers that these stories are fictitious, they should ignore such a hasty conclusion. Most of the incidents recorded here are based on actual events and Horatio was an actual person; although I have to admit to surrounding his character with some embellishments as to his origins and detailed behaviour.

That Horatio Evans was someone special is not in doubt; there are many men (mainly) like him. It is said that the male of each species is designed to pit himself against nature, to take risks, so as to advance the species and expand its skills. This may not have been precisely the motive driving Horatio but many of his actions and intentions could be expalained by such a forgiving description. In which case, he emerges as a hero.

In other instances, where he would pit himself against ridiculous odds, he may emerge as a simple idiot. I leave the reader to decide which fits him best overall. In whichever category he falls, the town where he established his family was never the same and stories of him continue to permeate the Welsh valley in which these scenes principally take place.

Horatio provided an inexhaustible source of interest, amusement and sometimes dread for the greater family of which he and I were members. And we all loved him.

Ray Noyes, 2015

Contents

A Hero is Born

HORATIO WAS BORN on a Tuesday, which is a happy coincidence, since Tuesdays were bin days in Llanelli: days that would be crucial to the lad much later in life. Little did his parents know the significance of the happy event that struck the Evans household on that day, in the year of his birth, 1939.

This year signified the outbreak of hostilities, not only between Prime Minister Neville Chamberlain and Reich Chancellor Adolf Hitler but also between Lavender Evans, Horatio's mother, and Arthur, his father; hostilities that were to have a profound effect on the life of Horatio Evans.

Arthur and Lavender were not well matched. He, a lowly wheel tapper in the local railway sidings came from humble Welsh stock and was proud of it. His bushy, Stalin moustache and semi-bald head reflected someone who was ordinary, someone content with his lot, not going anywhere soon.

True, tapping wheels was not going to get him very far, or stimulate his intellect much; but it was an important function and one he believed in. He had convinced himself that his work was a calling, not a job; otherwise he could not have stuck at it. He was sure that checking the soundness of a train's wheels was something that passengers using the Llanelli to Swansea line would be profoundly grateful for, if only they realised it was going on.

Some passengers may occasionally have wondered what the clang of his hammer signified as he struck each wheel in turn at Llanelli Station or at remote sidings, but he had long accepted that few did. He knew that his work was essential but unknown to the majority of passengers.

In spite of this, he managed to pull himself out of his marital bed each morning at 6.30 and make his way to the depot to pick up his long-handled hammer with its small head (a tool which resembled his own physiognomy, for he too was long in the body and small of head) and seek wheels on the carriages of trains to receive his careful and expert percussive ministrations. Such men made British Railways what it was, he told himself. There were no cracked wheels on the trains between Llanelli and Swansea just because of his expertise – surely this was worthwhile?

It had to be so, because those uncountable taps each day were his only defence against his darling wife. Without tapping wheels, his wife would be tapping him, taller and stronger as she was. In fact, Arthur only became fully Arthur when he was tapping wheels. Otherwise, he was just a humble serf, ruled over in their small two-up, two-down terraced house at number 34, Tinplate Terrace, by his darling wife, Lavender.

To Arthur, no two wheels were the same. Strange to say, that although healthy wheels were those that gave a pleasant, reassuring 'ring' when tapped, his inner rebel was always secretly and ashamedly delighted when he found one that responded with a dull clank. Like a thief, waiting for the opportunity to commit a crime, he would wait patiently with eager anticipation, listening to wheel after wheel, for that telling noise to sound out.

He'd found one! This finding of a defective wheel lifted his spirits as though he had committed a forbidden sin – and it was something his wife needn't know about either. It was his secret and his alone, until he took his yellow chalk and made a cross on the wheel, showing it had to be changed.

So although to the casual observer and to his rather liverish foreman, he was the diligent, honest tapper of wheels, the guardian of safe travel on the railway, he had a demon on his shoulder; one intent upon welcoming into its kingdom a wheel gone wrong. In fact, he had occasionally found himself hesitating about using that lump of yellow chalk; what if he ignored that cracked wheel? Oversights could happen, after all.

At such times he savoured at full strength the power he held in his hammer hand. But chalk it he did – always. His working class sense of honesty and the professional integrity of his craft would not allow him to be slipshod. (But it was a good, fleeting feeling, that sense of power.)

Lavender, on the other hand, came from different stock: her family, the Ffotheringay-Smythes were from Bristol, an altogether different milieu to Llanelli. They owned and ran a successful florist shop in the Clifton area of the city. Its name, 'Flowers for the Lady', was painted in gilt above a dark green shop-front in a posh area – one that could afford flowers. That their daughter should carry the name of Lavender was, to them, quite natural. (Her mother always told her that their surname, carrying as it did a double 'f' was a sign of their ancestral greatness: in truth, her great-great-grandfather had a bad stutter.)

How Lavender and Arthur got together (she never admitted to anything so common as falling in love) was, she reckoned – and kept pointing out, a mistake. They met in 1938, both aged 19, when they were visiting Bristol Zoo – she with her mother in a party from the WI, he with some mates from the Engineers' Arms in Llanelli.

She had become separated from the virginal ladies of the WI and was lost near the penguin enclosure. Arthur and his mates, however, were next door at the adjacent baboon enclosure, laughing at them doing rather disgusting things (the baboons, that is) when he noticed she was looking rather distraught – probably at what the baboons were doing, which was clearly visible from the clean, white and somewhat clinical penguin enclosure.

Wishing to save her blushes, he offered to find the WI group, to the amusement of the (amazingly) still-sober gentlemen from the Engineers' Arms, and led her to the information centre near the zoo entrance. The girl at the centre had already been alerted to Lavender's plight by the chairwoman of the WI party, a lady by the modest name of Boudicia, a name that encapsulated accurately her character.

Arthur was smitten! The rescue of this pretty damsel and the sexual exploits of the baboons had set his heart on fire. He asked her the universal question, 'Do you come here often?' He then committed what was probably the worst blunder of his entire life, convincing her he was a trainee design engineer who was taking a degree at Swansea University. She would love Swansea Bay, he insisted, and painted a picture of endless blue skies and clear blue water lapping at the shore – omitting to mention the sewage outlets.

In her darkest moments, Lavender admitted she was somewhat taken in by this 'working class' boy and his amusing Welsh accent – and cursed herself for it. But she was at a rebellious stage in her life and did not see why a fling with such a lad should not be fun. Thus she was tempted to catch a train to Swansea and meet him for a day on the beach. Now Swansea beach is very large and it hides a number of rocky nooks and crannies on its western side, in one of which their baby son was conceived.

She, of course, was not only shocked at being pregnant, but appalled that it should be by someone 'common'. Her 'bit of rough' had turned out to have a rather significant 'downside', his social milieu. Her parents were not only horrified, but eventually cast her aside, to pursue a future with Arthur on whatever terms he could offer. Good florists from Bristol would never contemplate doing what she'd done; she was an outcast, a mutant florist.

Everything was going wrong for her: her entirely false

professional design engineer, who on marriage gave her the all-too-short and (horrors!) Welsh name of Evans, was actually just a wheel-tapper. 'Why on earth did he have to be Welsh?' her parents wailed. Shame was not the emotion she felt: it was anger! He, Arthur Handel Elias Evans, was going to pay for this – throughout eternity.

Her first step in a lifelong campaign of revenge was to restore to the family some dignity by giving the child a decent name – no Dai, no Dick no Dylan would do; it had to be something that stood out and showed off her middle-class, English ancestry. Horatio Evans was born.

Arthur and his family were not happy either. His father was a fervent nationalist and didn't see why they 'should be cowering before the bloody English again'. Middle names were bandied about, the Ffotheringay-Smythes refusing to be involved at all, having told all their friends and relations that Lavender had suddenly emigrated to New Zealand with a brain surgeon she'd met at a church bring-and-buy sale.

Eventually, Arthur's father hit on a plan: if Arthur went along to the register office to register the birth alone, he could add whatever names he liked and Lavender could do nothing about it. And so it was that Arthur returned from the Llanelli registry office with a certificate that attested to the fact that he was the father of Horatio ap Llewelyn Evans. 'Let 'em stick that in their bloody florist's window!' proclaimed Arthur's father.

In defence of Arthur's deceit, he did resist committing a further misdemeanour, that of altering the child's surname by adding an 'ap' to that too, as suggested by his father; but Arthur judged it to be an assertion of Welshness too far and may even have been illegal. Besides, Horatio ap Llewelyn ap Evans would be one ap too far and would have made a real mouthful of his tiny son's name.

On Arthur's return from the registry office, Lavender asked

to see the certificate. Against all the odds, Arthur managed to convince her that he'd put it in the bank for safe-keeping. She couldn't prove anything, but her innate ability to read faces – especially guilty ones – (a skill undoubtedly inherited from her shop-keeping parents), made her feel intuitively uneasy.

Two days later her suspicions were confirmed when Arthur's father, never known for being tactful, asked her what she thought of the baby's names. The subsequent domestic scene was not a pretty one, as he recited them, slowly, placing particular emphasis on the baby's middle name of ap Llewelyn as he leaned into her face.

No-one had told her that the added 'ap' meant 'son of'. Few, if any, fathers of sons born since Prince Llewelyn's death in 1240 had had the effrontery to claim that their son was his true heir. This did not bother Arthur's dad, who if questioned about it would assert that it was 'about bloody time someone did then'.

Not only was Lavender understandably offended at being deceived, but she knew little of, and cared even less about, Welsh history, so that this middle name was simply ridiculous. Besides, she couldn't even spell it.

Tears were shed for weeks – and Arthur worked a lot of overtime. Little did he realise the effect that the alignment of his baby's name with a Welsh prince would have. The fact was, the world was not ready for Horatio ap Llewelyn Evans and the great expectations Lavender had of him. If her husband was a failure, her son was going to be a success. This was to be her revenge. Llanelli didn't know it yet, but it would have to prepare itself to welcome greatness, she said to herself.

His Formative Years

T HAT LAVENDER HAD married beneath her was something to which she could never become accustomed. And she was determined to ensure that her discomfort registered in most of what she did. Any attempt on her part to integrate into what she felt was a backward, Neolithic, druidic society was at best half-hearted and at worst determined to fail.

For example, try as she may, she could not bring herself to understand the emotions that arose in Arthur's breast when discussing wheel tapping. And as for inserting the merits of her husband's job into conversations with other women, into which she may have inadvertently been drawn, she could not contemplate it. Such 'common' women actually talked on doorsteps, a position no self-respecting housewife should occupy. 'Why don't they have afternoon tea indoors in the parlour?' she wondered. How she yearned for Bristol, although she was supposed to be in Christchurch, New Zealand, not that her parents had ever told her of their lie.

'Maybe none of these women has either a parlour or a tea set,' she wondered, ignoring that she was bereft of them too. Offering afternoon tea was certainly something her neighbours would never understand when they could just as easily (and cheaply) stand on their doorsteps in Tinplate Terrace and natter away, each nursing a 'liberated' British Railways mug.

So many were the offences offered to poor Lavender by this way of life that she was sometimes overwhelmed by them. She could see faults everywhere: faults in behaviour (what her mother would have called poor etiquette); faults in housekeeping (why were so many houses so dirty?); even faults in the shops which had, to her way of thinking, pathetically limited choices available and those of such poor quality.

An example of this occurred about six months into her stay at Llanelli. She decided to make one last attempt at being civilised and decided to cook Arthur a special meal. For this she needed spaghetti, natural, dried spaghetti, which she asked for at her usual grocer's. His reply floored her: 'Which one d'you want, bach, 'oops or alphabet?' She simply could not bring herself to buy a tin of either and walked home utterly dejected. Her final attempt at bringing sophistication to Tinplate Terrace had failed.

Her neighbours, whom she had once hoped would be a source of friendship, never rose to her high standards and so never made it to her pantheon. They even wore aprons (not always clean and sometimes torn) in the street; or they put their hair in curlers and wrapped their heads in scarves rather than having it 'put up' at the hairdresser's.

And so, very quickly, it dawned on Lavender that such things as those to which she had been accustomed – good quality fresh fruit, a weekly visit to the hairdresser and to a department store – were not only unaffordable for her neighbours, they were unavailable.

Llanelli was a little slow in catching up with these things. The worst part of it was when she realised they were not only unaffordable for the people of Llanelli, but for her too. This was the cruellest blow of all: she was now an ordinary Llanelli wife, with an ordinary Llanelli husband's wage packet.

The whole tenure of Llanelli life was an anathema to her. There was the language for one thing: not only did most neighbours, shopkeepers and the like, speak this alien, out-dated ancient language, but their English was appalling. The use of strange terms such as 'over by there' or 'we do do something' was so irritating that she refused to get used to it. Her relationship with the people of Llanelli was not improved by her pointing out how badly they spoke and even correcting them. As a result, she could not avoid hearing herself described as 'stuck up', accompanied by the question: 'Who does she think she is, the little madam?'

But perhaps the most annoying thing of all for her, which sent her neighbours (especially the women) into fits of laughter, was when Arthur called her 'Lav'. We can easily imagine that by now her neighbours fully understood her distain for life in Tinplate Terrace, so that the tag of Lav was just perfect for her. Even when Arthur tried to soften the term of affection by adding 'bach' it didn't really work. Everyone knew that the Rubicon had been crossed – not least dear Lavender herself. She was marooned in Llanelli. There was only one solution for her: to maintain a dignified distance between herself and the people of Llanelli by staying indoors, closing her front door to the horrid world outside and trying her utmost to maintain her higher standards.

And so it happened that Lavender devoted all her attention to tutoring Horatio – indoors. She refused to use his middle names, finding difficulty in pronouncing its double 'l' in Llewelyn and dropped the 'ap' as an unnecessary and worthless appendage. She intended that he should be 'a somebody', someone of whom she could be proud. Her intentions were good, but once again she was thwarted by the practicalities of such a scheme.

But time went on and the baby grew. Horatio began school at the age of five with all his peers. The poor lad, however, had never learned to be street-wise and look after himself, corralled as he was indoors with his mother. But he learned fast to defend himself, often with his fists.

Here we see for the first time the essential elements of his character emerging – he was becoming a fighter. Even at such a tender age he often returned home with bruises and cuts after 'sorting out' another child or two. If Lavender had given up, he hadn't. His Llanelli life was only just beginning. He was becoming a Llanelli boy. His father, of course, was delighted. What a lad! Very proud he was, but not dear Lavender. Was further shame to be heaped upon her head by having a son who resolved disagreements with his fists?

The school, however, was not at all alarmed at Horatio's pugnacious character and felt that he was simply showing some 'character', some spirit. It was this very character that was to help him in later life as we shall see. He was destined to be a fighter of causes – most of them lost, but causes nevertheless. Some would later say he became a fighter without a cause, to the point where many people never understood why he was always in such a campaigning mood when everything around them seemed so peaceful and calm. It would seem that Horatio could make an issue out of anything, even those things that seemed to be running perfectly smoothly to the ordinary voter.

***

We now skip some years to when Horatio left school. His application to subjects academic had not been blindingly successful and he was advised, if not pushed (some say the headmaster begged), into leaving school and taking up a job. Once again, his mother resisted such a crass idea and felt that if only he could attend a better school, all would be well. But it was not to be. There were no better schools on the doorstep and anyway the fees would be unaffordable.

Arthur took the hint when the headmaster called him in one day and offered to pay him (bribe him?) from his own pocket if Horatio were removed from beneath the hallowed roofs of the Llanelli Council Junior Mixed School, Offal Road,

Llanelli. Of course Arthur did not tell his wife the full details of the interview, or of their son's resultant exit from the learned establishment; Arthur had accepted by then the need to dress up facts in sweeter, more positive terms for her absorption. He therefore told her that the headmaster believed that Horatio was far too advanced for his years and would be less bored by having a job.

If it hadn't been for her neighbours hinting at the real reason, she may have believed Arthur's story, but gradually the truth filtered through. She was furious with Arthur. As punishment, Arthur was not allowed in the marital bed, or even the house, for several days for this lie, a period which he thoroughly enjoyed, living as he did throughout this enforced period of penury and banishment in the warm, friendly glow of the engine sheds. (How he later yearned for further enforced holidays of this sort, but few were to come his way.)

More disappointment for Lavender was to follow. Her son was to walk in his father's footsteps in pursuing a career in transport. In Horatio's case, it was road transport. He achieved this in a roundabout way via the army. Although he missed being called up for the war, he had to do a year's national service. He felt that his character which, it has to be admitted, had by now become primarily belligerent, was perfectly fitted for such a career. He'd also developed a rather loud voice and a tendency to emphasise his arguments by aid of a finger that prodded the air alarmingly and sometimes poked the listener in the chest. He could certainly get his point across, even if it was invalid.

The recruitment office in Llanelli High Street was initially delighted that they had a customer, even one that had been called up. But as the initial interview proceeded doubts about the new recruit were expressed, behind closed doors. He told them he was glad to answer the call because he had clear leadership potential, seeing himself quite soon as a regimental sergeant major, shouting across the parade ground to his battalion, a stickler for discipline and standing no nonsense from anyone. He told them confidently that given a little time he intended rising through the ranks to become a senior officer, perhaps gaining a VC in some war or other (perhaps one he'd started). But the army didn't want him to join as a driver of men – they insisted he be a driver of lorries.

It is difficult to say whether the army forged his character, or simply enhanced it; because his army service produced someone who was confident, strident, independent, and, it has to be admitted, still belligerent. It was reckoned that his (self-acclaimed) knowledge of the law was one of his strong points and numerous were the occasions when he cited chapter and verse of army regulations at his corporal in order to get around completing some task or other – either on his own behalf or that of others in his company. He had become the barrack room lawyer.

This feature of his character, defending his own rights and the rights of others, tempted him to start up an army trade union, but his commanding officer didn't think too much of the idea. (This was an idea Horatio was to take up later when he returned to civilian life. Trade Unionism felt like a good area in which he could specialise and use his undoubted talents of political persuasion and leadership.) It is not difficult to imagine that he was not the nearest and dearest friend of the company sergeant. The poor man gradually lost his nerve completely and was committed to an asylum suffering from nervous exhaustion and shellshock – although he hadn't been anywhere near shells; he'd just been near Horatio, but the effect on the poor man was the same.

Efforts to have Horatio removed early from the army failed, even when he appeared to have been caught red-handed doing dodgy deals; he was constantly thinking up schemes for outwitting the military authorities. As complaints about him escalated further and further up the chain of command, it became apparent that much time was being wasted by ever more senior people in simply getting Horatio just to drive his lorry and keep away from trouble.

His success at siphoning off literally thousands of gallons of diesel for the black market did not endear him to the authorities, although they were shocked at how easy he made it seem and as a result tightened up their security procedures for storing fuel.

When threatened with a full court martial, Horatio remained undaunted. He argued that if he was able to make the military authorities aware of how poor their security procedures were, perhaps he could be employed (at a higher rank) as a security consultant. He could have a bash at other schemes too and help them reveal weaknesses in their procedures.

'I'd be doing you buggers a favour,' he asserted to the tribunal chairman in court. 'Just you think about it, boyo, I've offered you a bloody good deal and it's staring you in the face, mun.'

But the chairman of the military tribunal was not amused and the poor man had certainly never been addressed as 'boyo' or 'mun' – strange terms that he asked be translated for him. In fact, Horatio's suggestion and the way he expressed it may have contributed to the tribunal chairman's decision to hand over the case to someone else whilst he took a break for the good of his blood pressure. [The reader may recognise similarities between Horatio's behaviour and those of the character Just William in all this. They were quite alike, albeit of different social classes.]

As often happens in cases where the rule book doesn't seem to be of any help in controlling such people, promoting them can sometimes be a solution, especially if promoted to something banal, safe and of no consequence. There were therefore whispered suggestions (albeit behind closed doors accompanied by much smoke and uncounted glasses of whisky) that Horatio be promoted.

At first the suggestion was not only laughed at but totally ignored. It was so incredible that it surely could not have been made seriously. The very idea of giving Private Horatio more power was so frightening to those valiant men in his chain of command that it was the final trigger for the sergeant's enforced commitment to the asylum. Getting the demented sergeant out of the ammunition store where he had locked himself for two days, without destroying half of Swansea was, it was later admitted, touch and go.

But weird things can happen and they seemed to happen pretty often to Horatio. Within the year he was indeed promoted – becoming Lance corporal Evans, Fuel Supplies – or as his peers called him 'Evans the Juice'. This unfortunate nickname, which referred to his conviction for siphoning off fuel, was one he was strangely proud of, although it was really meant as a dig by his mates at his conviction for stealing.

Unfortunately, nicknames cannot be used by authority figures such as a commanding officer. But the colonel was determined to get his own back on Horatio and bided his time, waiting until he could use his ultimate weapon: writing out Horatio's final discharge papers, including a personal reference.

The colonel wrote a verbose essay describing the extraordinary and unnerving talents, of Lance corporal Evans, H ap Ll, number 862457. His soldier's record book containing his colonel's parting 'love letter' as Horatio described it, ran to three additional pages plus an appendix, ending in sincere wishes that 'We hope he'll go far'. (The colonel's hand shook as he placed the full stop after the word 'far', because he really, desperately wanted to add the word 'away'.) Horatio, reading the colonel's notes felt rather proud: 'Well, he might be a stuck-up English knob, but he's taken a lot of trouble with this and I'm bloody proud to have served under him.'

Our hero now saw a bright future for himself in civilian life; the army had certainly noticed him and he was determined to fulfil his potential. Even if the rest of the world saw his actions as odd, even disturbing, he felt he was treading a new, enlightened path, one that would confront injustice and banality at every turn.

The army did have some positive effects on him. He left with a more upright, some might even say arrogant, appearance. He held his chin up and wore a trilby hat rather than a flat cap. The trilby was tilted at a rakish angle, something for which he would be known for the rest of his life. He even stuck a pheasant's feather in it for good measure. In fact, so devoted was he to wearing a hat, he was hardly ever seen without one; he always wore one in the house, even at meals. If he was hatless, he was either ill or dead.

He also took to shining his shoes, although this stopped pretty quickly after he took his first job, where he was required to wear industrial, steel-capped boots. 'If I polishes these boots I'll look like a bloody copper,' he reasoned. 'Besides which, it's too middle class to have shiny shoes.' This type of thinking was one of the earliest signs of his burgeoning politicisation, which soon saw him joining the Llanelli branch of the Communist Party.

To help him fit in with such an organisation, he grew a moustache, but thinner and sharper than his father's. His moustache, and the cocked hat with its feather, defined him somehow. He felt he looked like someone who was going places, even if he didn't have a clue where that might be.

Taking the Wheel

O NCE DISCHARGED (SOME say ejected) from his short stay in the army, Horatio launched himself into society armed with a particular skill: driving lorries. He loved them. If there was one thing that fired up his enthusiasm and lit up his eyes, it was a lorry. In his quieter moments of self-analysis, he admitted that being up high – above the crowd as it were – was his destiny; his rightful place, physically and metaphorically.

And it didn't matter what type, shape or function of lorry he drove – everything from long-distance articulated juggernauts to ash carts. Luckily for him, he didn't mind the latter because that is where he found his true calling. For him, driving an ash cart was a vocation: ridding society of its detritus was a social benefit he was proud to perform as a true communist. He wasn't only a collector of rubbish, he was also a saviour: of things unwanted and unloved, as we shall see.

But we're getting ahead of ourselves. At the age of 27 he married a slender girl by the name of Gladys who came from Abertwp in the Swansea Valley. She was taller than him and of the same age, but frail. She appeared to suffer a number of unidentifiable illnesses, all of which were mysterious and imminently life-threatening. Hardly any were known to science. For years her life expectancy remained a matter of months.

Visitors to her parents' house learned quickly not to enquire after her health. Asking 'How are you, dear?' was fatal, because they'd be told – in horrifying detail. The symptoms then described would be distressing to the faint-hearted, requiring them to drink several cups of sweet tea (sometimes with brandy) to recover from the shock. Many a visitor left the cottage pale and shaky; symptoms like Gladys's were not only unusual but terrifyingly upsetting. 'She won't last long, poor love. She's a martyr, she is, a martyr,' was the usual thought.

Gladys was one of numerous brothers and sisters, all of whom remained in the valley once they'd married. Horatio found that by tying the knot with Gladys he'd become a member of a rather large family. This cheered him. He, an only child, had missed out on siblings, uncles and aunts. His mother refused to let her Bristol family meet him; his father was an only child too. So here, in the mining valley of Abertwp, was a ready-made family for him and as it turned out, a ready-made audience for his schemes, theories and politics.

Their marriage was not without its problems: the wedding ceremony itself being the very first. Horatio, although a solid member by now of the working class, had strong beliefs to do with all things social and spiritual. In short, he was against them.

He felt that the accepted precepts of society were there to be challenged and in this he found his calling – one of several, in fact – which he embraced with vigour throughout his adult life.

This Quixotic side to his character was to get him into trouble, but trouble out of which he always seemed to slip. Unlike Don Quixote, he wasn't a well-read, titled gentleman but this didn't stop the comparison being made by all who encountered him. One has to wonder what influence his name, Horatio, may have had on his willingness to confront dragons and evil-doers of all sorts, real or imagined, political or social.

Meanwhile, the wedding had to be planned. One thing they could agree upon was that it should take place in Abertwp.

Lavender, didn't actually say she didn't want it in Llanelli where the neighbours would meet Gladys and her mining family, but the choice of somewhere other than Llanelli did give her some relief from her chronic social embarrassment.

Gladys wanted a simple, chapel wedding with just her family present. Horatio, always conscious of the need to promote the cause of the proletariat, wanted a civil ceremony, however, attended by the Brethren from the Communist Party.

He insisted on having as witnesses an additional cohort drawn from the 'Buffs' – the Royal Antediluvian Order of Buffaloes – which he had also joined when living in Llanelli. At the time of the wedding, he was just a junior Buffalo – a Calf in fact – but he had great expectations of moving up to the First Degree of Wallaby and even becoming the Great Bison (fourth degree) one day. Imagining himself in the full regalia of the Great Bison, sitting in the Master's chair at banquets, filled him with ambitious pleasure. But he harboured doubts as to whether Gladys would be up to being Lady Great Bison – or was it the Great Lady Bison, he wasn't sure.

It has to be said, that his brother Communists were not too happy about his membership of the Buffs. The Buffaloes were so middle class and bourgeois that two of the Brethren suggested pointedly that Horatio should choose one or other organisation. But he was one of those exceptional leaders who can convince members of the proletariat one day and members of the middle classes the next that he was one of them – both at the same time.

One sees at once a clash of ideology: Gladys wanting no fuss, a simple chapel ceremony with family and friends; Horatio was going for the Full Monty – representatives of two worldwide organisations: the Communist Party and the Buffaloes would be there, and Gladys should be honoured, as he was, that they'd agreed to come.

But love conquers all – and Gladys gave in. The Brethren turned up in numbers, some carrying red flags and all expecting a free lunch at the Bomb and Dagger pub, and filled most of the front seats, as though to assert their rights as the inheritors of the Earth. The Buffaloes filled the back of the chapel resplendent in their regalia. Gladys managed to have her preferred venue at least.

There were just a few details that Horatio failed to negotiate with Gladys, her family and the presiding preacher: he was not allowed to wear his Buffalo regalia or his Communist beret during the ceremony, nor was he allowed a phalanx of red Communist flags under which to walk when exiting the chapel. And the organist refused to play 'The Internationale'. Otherwise, he was a happy man.

The sandwiches at the Bomb and Dagger were not as soggy as had usually been experienced and some of those described as beef even contained meat. The beer was excellent and was amazingly close, for once, to its legal specific gravity. Geraint, the landlord, had clearly put on quite a show for Horatio.

'Put on a special, proper brew for you 'Or,' he had said, as though accepting that his brew wasn't always what it should have been. (It was just as well that Lavender did not hear her son's name being shortened to 'Or' or her despairingly negative view of all things Welsh would have been complete.)

The Communist Brethren were suitably impressed by the 'do', especially as it was free, and their numbers strangely increased above that counted in the chapel; until a fight broke out in the car park between a Party member and two stray Buffaloes who asserted loudly that capitalism was here to stay and Communism was done for.

'Why don't you Commies just pack up and bugger off?' they suggested. The Brethren were not amused.

'These bloody bourgeois Buffaloes are taking the piss out of the People's Revolution!' one of them cried. 'They ought to feel what it's like when the workers rise up – let's show 'em, boys!'

It was a somewhat degrading quarrel in which senior Buffaloes should involve themselves, particularly with one of them being of the Second Degree (Kangaroo) and the other the Alderman of Benevolence (First Class) which, next to the Great Bison is the highest rank. Nevertheless, having been attacked, they gave a good account of themselves.

A third Buffalo would like to have taken part, but his office as the Certified Primo, Third Degree of the Great Marmot prevented his engagement. So he watched from behind a door of the outside toilets.

In the end, brute force from the Brethren (and the hampering effect of smart suits and the Buffaloes' clanging regalia) began to turn the fight in the Brethren's favour. Regalia was ripped from two Buffaloes and the medal of the Degree of the Kangaroo was tossed into a bank of stinging nettles. But the Buffaloes' revenge was sweet as they captured not only the Communist red flag (resplendent with hammer and sickle) but also a Brother's beret (complete with red enamelled star). The flag had been fixed to the car park gatepost, arousing much curiosity from nearby residents, some of whom believed the long-awaited Welsh uprising was underway.

Dai Bungalow (so named because he had nothing upstairs), who helped in the Post Office, was certain of it. He began preparations for the revolution by turning the Queen's portrait to face the wall, something he'd been dying to do for years, but resisted, in case it gave the game away that he had nationalist 'leanings' when working for Her Majesty's Civil Service. 'I've been licking that woman's bloody stamps for 14 years; surely it's time to have our own back?'

It was clear from the way that the Buffaloes and Brethren fought, that poor Horatio was in a cleft stick; he belonged to both sides. But here was where his leadership skills came in; he called down shame on both camps and urged them back inside the Bomb and Dagger to resume the celebrations.

But his pleadings did not meet with an immediate ceasefire, which was a bit of a shame. Hostilities were strangely self-perpetuating; but calm did resume after several Buffaloes (led by Brother Kangaroo) drove off at speed, pursued uselessly by a few of the Communist Brethren who only had bikes.

At around 1 a.m. the following morning, the wedding breakfast came to a drunken end. In this state it was now impossible to recognise a Buffalo from a Brother. All had shed their jackets, ties, and anything else setting them aside from the common man and were snoring away either on the floor or slumped in chairs. In fact, several deep relationships had been unwittingly forged between a Buffalo and a Brother, all of which would be a source of some shame in the daylight.

*

The following day Horatio had time for contemplation, as the healing process from the night before slowly took place, aided by large doses of Alka Seltzer. He realised that although he had been close to his father, and like him recognised his place in society, he was different thanks to his special gift. He just knew he had inherited a latent leadership gene from his mother.

Just as Lavender and her colonial English family felt their lives were to be lived out answering a higher calling than that of the working class, namely, that they born to lead; so, somewhere in Horatio's genome was a sneaky little trait that expressed the self-same characteristic.

This presented a problem for him: how to use this inherited gene in an otherwise modest working class environment? How to be a leader for the Buffs and another for the Brethren? But why, he realised, should he limit his ambitions to those organisations? The whole of Abertwp society needed a shake-up and there was no reason why he shouldn't be the man to do it.

'Needs a bloody bomb under it, this place does,' was an observation he frequently made to whoever, willing or otherwise, would listen. He didn't like Abertwp very much. It was too enclosed for him, too small a stage on which to strut. Mining was the main occupation, except for jobs on the Abertwp Council, the slaughterhouse, or the toilet bowl factory; and things ground rather slowly there. In fact nothing much happened at all. Time ground even more slowly than in Llanelli. (An indication of this sleepy approach to life was a headline in the Abertwp Herald: 'Police Constable Loses Whistle – Enquiry Underway.') It needed shaking up.

Thus it was, that although Gladys, her parents and siblings were relatively content with their lot in Abertwp and the nearby mining villages, Horatio judged them to be the downtrodden lackeys, slaves even, of rich, exploitative, capitalist employers – many of them colonial English, which was, in his eyes, the most profound condemnation of all.

He went so far as to imply (if that isn't too mild a term for the language he actually employed) that they should be ashamed of themselves for accepting such an awful yoke. A capitalist society was, for him, something inherently evil that had to be confronted. He was the man destined to do it. Confronting the global evil of capitalism was to be his sacred calling. And it would start in Abertwp – why not?

'Gotta start somewhere!' He would say. 'Karl Marx did, in the British Library – mind you, we 'aven't even got a library.'

Since his thinking was now reaching a higher, more strategic level (defeating global capitalism single-handedly is pretty strategic), he developed certain mannerisms that set him apart from the common man (unfortunately). Many great leaders did this, he argued. They spoke in a certain way, or dressed differently. They have notable mannerisms quite often.

His chosen mannerism was to place an ever greater emphasis on his existing habit of poking the air when excited, which came to the fore when pontificating on political issues. He decided to enhance this eccentricity so that it became his trademark.

Seeing him on the High Street even from a distance, people could tell if he was trying to convince some poor voter of the need for change. His finger would be jabbing the air and the listener, whose posture was always that of leaning backwards as far as possible, was clearly trying to get out of the way, blinking his eyes as he did so. Indeed, some listeners would become alarmed, in case that finger penetrated an eye, as Horatio ap Llewelyn Evans leaned in closer to the listener's face to make his point, spraying his unfortunate victim with just a little spit as his thin moustache began to twitch.

Poor Gladys, meanwhile, who was a simple soul, was not ready for this burgeoning of her husband's leadership talents or his eccentricities, natural or artificial. She was completely lost – often distressed – at his thundering political diatribes (which were particularly loud in their small cottage) and just wished for a quiet life with which to bring up her two girls and nurse her mysterious ailments.

She also wished to be able to get on quietly with consuming her Woodbines in peace, which was very difficult since Horatio declared he didn't like people who smoked – not because it was unhealthy or made the house smell, but he believed cigarettes were made by capitalists in order to drug the poor and keep them under control.

In a Communist Party meeting he once declared: 'The workers are in eternal servitude to bloody capitalist fags and are paying the price.' To which one of the Brethren disrespectfully shouted, 'Yes, they're three-and-bloody-seven now; they used to be two bob for twenty.'

The two girls were Gladys' pride and joy and, to be fair, that of their father too. He was a proud man and they were another layer of pride to add to his growing achievements. But they presented him with a dilemma: he wanted them to have a good education and all the signs were that they were worthy of one; but what if they married someone from the managerial class? What if they even became professional people and took on the mantle of employers themselves?

This needed watching! The Brethren of the Abertwp Communist Party (South Wales Region, Swansea Valley Division) would also be watching. Heavy is the (domestic) burden of leadership.

In a well-intended attempt to keep his girls on the straight and narrow, Horatio nailed a framed motto above the mantelpiece in their bedroom that read, rather menacingly: 'Thou Shalt Not.' It was an embroidered 'tester' that some virginal young lady had painstakingly made many years ago. It was very faded and badly-stained due to the rain and the seagull droppings falling on it as it looked Heavenwards on the local tip. The outcome was that the faded admonition now read: 'Thou Shalt No'.

The girls promised their father they would always do this, whatever it was.

Horatio was not a man to split hairs and accepted their vow.

Councillor
Horatio Evans

H<small>ORATIO'S NATURAL GIFTS</small> as a leader were to emerge into the full light of day when he was elected to the town council. He had expected a chain of office, but was told he would have to wait until he became mayor. One of the Communist Party Brethren pointed out that all were equal under communism and he should shun anything that placed him above his brothers and sisters, such as a chain of office.

Horatio asserted that he'd only wanted a chain on behalf of the Brethren, but it didn't sound convincing. (It goes to show that whereas we are all equal, some are more equal than others.) Notwithstanding the disappointment of having no regalia, he was prepared to give of his valuable time and energy for the good of the town of Abertwp.

We all know that there are a few essential services that councils need to focus on: one is waste collection and another is the position and number of public toilets. The Brethren were particularly keen to install some of the latter because, they said, it would directly assist the suffering of workers in society.

Horatio's approach was similar, but different. He had been waging a personal campaign against capitalism for years, by relieving himself against the side door of the bank whenever he could, usually at night of course. This act of urinary rebellion gave him a singular political as well as physiological pleasure.

Peeing on an icon of capitalism was an especially delightful experience.

Because of this campaign, and his long-time habit of picking up discarded items from back lanes and 'saving' them, he felt singularly qualified to offer advice in both specialist fields: the positioning of urinals and waste management. In the latter because he had recently joined the honoured ranks of refuse collectors and in the latter because he experienced at first hand the discomfort provided by trying to walk home with a full bladder after an evening at the Buffaloes, where beer is the main attraction.

Meanwhile, his love of lorries had finally paid off. He found himself seated literally in the driving seat of a new multipurpose ash cart. It gave him a certain amount of power; after all it was he who determined the direction in which the thing would go: another dimension to his burgeoning leadership role in society.

Actually, if there was one thing that would annoy him it would be for his vehicle to be described as an ash cart: it was a Waste Collection and Disposal Vehicle (Volvo Mk IV). He was generally pleased with it, but was quick to point out to his supervisor that the new Mark V had a number of features on it that he preferred and that if a suitable occasion should present itself, he would appreciate having one. The response of his supervisor has not been recorded, but it seems to have been pretty short.

The reader may pick up echoes of his stay in the army, and, sad to say, his supervisor was not long in being given long-term sick leave for his nerves. They say he never fully recovered, but is reasonably content to be living well away from the Abertwp depot, somewhere in Northumberland, in a nursing home. It is said he is a broken man. Bin day at the home is on a Friday and he has to be sedated most of the day.

More of the adventures of Horatio and his lorry later, but for now we should pay attention to Horatio's input to the location and the number of public loos, with particular attention to the route from the Masonic Hall, used by the Buffaloes, to his small terraced cottage.

It was entirely coincidental that two new urinals were installed between these two points during Horatio's term of office – to the 'relief' of many Buffaloes. Some Buffalo colleagues were so grateful, they suggested the urinals be named the Horatio ap Llewelyn Evans Urinals.

But his sense of pride and perhaps even a certain civic shyness (that wasn't always apparent), decided him against his name being cast indelibly and eternally in iron alongside the word 'urinal'. 'The Evans Urinal' or 'This Urinal was Erected by Horatio ap Ll Evans' didn't seem right somehow. He'd rather be remembered for something less common and smelly. Given time, he'd think of something suitable with which the town could thank him for his achievements. An opera house perhaps?

There were a few women councillors who raised a stink about the urinals, as if they didn't stink enough (the urinals, that is). They felt they had a good case for one of the two toilets being for women; but they were defeated in a mass show of hands (many of which had never been seen in the council chamber before, although they had been seen in the Communist Party Social Club) that outnumbered the women's 12 votes, by 49 (this, in spite of the total number of councillors being only 37).

And so, two new men's urinals were erected in Abertwp. One was about 200 yards from the Masonic Hall and the other about 200 yards from the Bomb and Dagger, both of which were about 200 yards from where Horatio lived, at 74 Slaughterhouse Terrace.

The geometric, surprisingly triangular, coincidence that these urinary equidistant positions presented to an observant voter was amazing. As one keen-eyed member of the electorate pointed out, the distance between the Buffaloes' meeting place and 74 Slaughterhouse Terrace just happened to be exactly the same as the distance between Slaughterhouse Terrace and the Bomb and Dagger. That the two new installations would be equidistant between Councillor Evans' two watering holes and his home was claimed to be purely coincidental. This assertion was made by the Council's anonymous spokesman (actually Horatio ap Llewelyn Evans) when interviewed by a reporter from the Abertwp Herald.

The minutes of the council meeting at which these facilities were approved, recorded that Councillor H ap Ll Evans spoke inspiringly and emotionally about the 'painful' need for these installations and called upon the council to 'pass' a motion, which it did.

Judging by the number of voters in the council building in support of the motion, it had to be passed in order to avoid a riot. The public balcony was packed to overflowing and the size of the crowd outside was intimidating. Most of them were waving red flags and chanting 'We'll Keep the Red Flag Flying'. Others, who didn't know the words, just sang 'We'll Keep a Welcome in the Hillsides' which strangely fitted the tune, more or less.

So the Brethren had once again won the day, which shows the power of democracy. As for improvements to the waste collection service of the town, these were to take place gradually as Horatio gained experience whilst piloting his Mark IV around the streets.

But in as much as his initial interest lay in discovering improvements that could be made, he very soon understood that the current method was in fact flawless; that is to say, it allowed the maximum amount of refuse to be collected in the shortest time whilst still allowing opportunities for the in-vehicle Mk IV crew to take initiatives of their own, such as personally 'recycling' some of it – an admirable achievement.

Horatio's understanding of the term 'recycling' was actually much more advanced than the classical one: he and the two other 'in-vehicle crew members' of the Horatio Express (as he named it) trained themselves to take note of items thrown out, usually in back lanes, and rather than see them buried in the local tip, they were 'rescued' and found new homes. This was true Communist recycling in action.

Consequently, there were a number of rescued items to be found in the homes of the Mk IV in-vehicle crew members, always, of course put to good use; to understand which, needs a visit to Horatio's home – to take but one example out of the three homes involved in the innovative recycling scheme in Abertwp.

The Conservatory

THE EVANS FAMILY home at 74 Slaughterhouse Terrace was a modest, vernacular dwelling in a group of ten terraced cottages. They had been built in the middle of the 19th century and consisted of just two rooms up and two rooms down. It can be imagined that in order to house (and sleep) the family of four, space was at a premium. So Horatio was always puzzling over ways of expanding the 'Abertwp Kremlin'.

One way was to construct a lean-to or conservatory out the back, protruding into the garden. There was enough room between the back of the house and the 'privy' to construct such a thing and he determined to set about it.

It often happens that a man endowed with gifts of the intellect is not well endowed with practical skills. This is not a firm and fast rule, but in Horatio's case it was absolutely true. He may have had a leadership gene, but other elements of his genome were lacking, notably the one for building things. This, of course, he couldn't possibly be expected to know, but Gladys had often told him he had something missing.

Unfortunately, leaders are often those who can throw themselves enthusiastically into the most insane and impossible projects in their determination to achieve their 'vision'. Napoleon and Hitler spring to mind. Horatio's vision was just the same: enthusiasm he possessed, suitable skills he did not. Events often conspire to defeat such people.

The outcome of his project was therefore rather different to that which he had envisaged. More to the point, it was dramatically different to the vision (nay, the Heavenly scenarios) described and promised to his dear wife and daughters. These disappointments affected Gladys's health; not only because of the chaotic disruption to the home, but because she consumed significantly more Woodbines on such occasions.

In the particular case described, the family was promised, and all imagined, having a beautiful glass conservatory under which they would leisurely take their breakfasts, luxuriating in the new, bright space Horatio had created. The sun would shine on them through the brilliant glass ceiling and they would be blissfully content as they looked out onto the runner beans and potatoes growing at the back of the house.

The result was just a little different.

Horatio had developed his dream of a new conservatory in some detail, but refused steadfastly to contemplate someone else building it. Above all, he could not stomach the notion of actually buying any part of it – not even a single brick. All could be found around back lanes, on the council tip – crying out to be 'recycled'.

The new edifice would have a glass ceiling of course and windows all round, sitting astride a low brick wall – an admirable and traditional design. In this case, it would not only provide a place to sit, cook and eat, but one in which to have a bath. The multipurpose aspects of it were inspirational.

All he needed were the parts and a little effort and he'd have just the thing to enhance the property in which he and the family lived. 'I'm not paying any bugger to build this; I'll do it for nowt,' was the approach he adopted with admirable optimism. 'Why put workers' money into the pockets of bloody capitalists when we can do it ourselves?' he reasoned.

It must be admitted, however, that neither his wife nor the two girls shared his optimism; they even tried to dissuade him from the project, based on previous schemes of his that had all started out like this, but had inevitably resulted in near disaster. What they realised with growing anxiety, verging on hysteria, was that never before had he attempted anything so large and so ambitious. When he erected a shelf that regularly fell off the wall, it was as nothing compared with a house extension.

The scheme would need alterations to the very structure of the house, not to mention plumbing and electrics of a fairly sophisticated nature. Optimism in the family seemed to have taken flight and was 'rapidly disappearing over the horizon with its arse on fire', observed a neighbour.

In the little house in Slaughterhouse Terrace the atmosphere was tense and gloomy; but leaders rise above such things and Horatio's spirit was on the rise: 'I'm always worried when Dad's in this optimistic mood', said the eldest daughter; 'I think I'll move out to somewhere safe. Why can't he just be lazy like other dads?'

The first thing Horatio had to do was to see how many bricks he might be able to find with which to construct low, stout walls for the base. From such a firm foundation he would add a timber frame and glaze it. All pretty simple, really. Oh, and he'd need a water supply of course, and the odd bit of electricity, oh, and drainage and perhaps even heating. The list was getting longer than he first thought, but undeterred he continued scouring the detritus and junk of the town to find what he'd need.

The problem with such a varied source of material is that each little piece could well be rather different to all the other little pieces, making for a rather higgledy-piggledy effect; and in the worst-case scenario, the pieces just won't fit together at all.

This is particularly true of plumbing materials. Joining an old lump of Victorian lead pipe to a piece of relatively modern copper pipe is not easy, especially if many such 'bits' (often each no more than six inches long) are all that can be found, requiring many of them to make up anything like a decent length through which water might be persuaded to flow. Making such a hybrid, multi-jointed pipe carry explosive gas under pressure was another obstacle which he hadn't overcome – yet.

One thing he was determined to avoid was buying anything new and of the right length; all would be found lying around in the back lanes of the town. It'd just need a little time to collect it, that's all.

Bricks for the low walls weren't too much of a problem: the cement to stick them together was – at least until he found three bags that had been thrown out of a building site. The bags seemed a little hard, but surely that's what cement is for, to go hard. So they were incorporated into his dream.

One fine day, he had amassed a sufficient number of bricks that had been painstakingly carried through the house (it had no rear access, everything had to be wheel-barrowed through the living room) and he was ready to start work.

The sand was easy: he got it from Swansea beach. 'A bit o' salt never 'urt no-one and the bloody stuff's free.' (It should be noted that an article in the Swansea Post that week expressed puzzlement that an Abertwp Council Mk IV ash cart was spotted at low tide being loaded with sand by three employees. The Council (actually Horatio himself, as a councillor, writing on Council notepaper) responded by pointing out that the promotion of good relations amongst ash cart teams of the two towns was a good thing and was encouraged by the latest EU directive on recycling. Flying the Abertwp flag on Swansea's beach was all part of that. No reason for the large hole left in the beach was advanced by the article.)

Eager to start and even more eager to finish, he decided against digging up what he considered the rather attractive and solid York Stone paving at the back of the house and digging foundations; having jumped up and down on the flagstones a couple of times, he declared:

'Solid as a rock, better than any bloody foundations. They knew what they were doing when they laid these things.' Foundations were therefore declared unnecessary. This was yet another example of his deep insight into all things structural.

We needn't follow his construction technique brick by brick, suffice it to conclude that the edifice was 'interesting' to say the least. Unconstrained by the need for straight lines or verticals, the walls were consequently an approximation to the base of a conservatory. Any changes to levels or to ensure straight lines would be made when he fixed the wooden structure on top of it, Horatio reasoned.

'That's the mistake too many bricklayers make,' he asserted, 'they're too keen on levels too early. The best place for getting it level is at the end, not at the beginning. That's what everyone sees after all, the finished job.' Which seemed strangely logical to his mates and poor Gladys, but they couldn't figure out why.

Wood was easy to find, but straight, workable wood was not. The timber he'd found was not of the latter category; but ever inventive, he used what he could get. This meant that different sections, lengths and strengths were blended together into an eccentric structure, which also incorporated windows that had appeared in back lanes and on tips. Being of different sizes, these windows required a creativity of which many carpenters could only dream. The net result was not so much a lean-to, as a 'lean-over'. Bulges here and there merely added to a work that spoke of creativity of the highest order. And it hadn't cost him a penny.

Why use modern double-glazed units for the roof when old windows would do? After all, they were made to last: 'Not like the bloody nasty stuff today; they knew how to make windows when these were made.' The fact that no matter how well made they had been they were not intended to be used as part of a conservatory roof was of course a minor weakness in his argument. Sash windows, especially, disliked being installed almost horizontally.

It was not to be expected that such an eccentric structure was either strong or waterproof, but it had a certain attraction, especially to people who live in yurts, tents, tepees, grass huts or similar curvilinear structures. The absence of true verticals, straight lines or horizontals was actually praised by Horatio as an indication of its uniqueness. 'Ask any surveyor and he'll tell you how difficult it is to build something that isn't straight.' He was right, of course.

This concept of the curvilinear 'added value' incorporated into the design was something lost on Gladys and the girls; but was a source of boasting by Horatio, especially when the structure which, it has to be said was becoming notorious across the town, was inspected by his communist Brethren and, more importantly, members of the Antediluvian Order of Buffaloes.

The ceremonies of the latter, it is well known, emulate the building of holy temples in ancient Egypt, so that verticals, horizontals and building skills in general are of great interest to them.

As far as the Communist brethren were concerned, the lean-over was a proletariat masterpiece: a fine example of the working class's struggle against capitalist property-owning bourgeoisie methods of construction.

The downside of this random structure was that the inside failed to present a straight surface of any kind against which to construct, say, a kitchen counter or a seat, or against which to place any item of furniture. But, undaunted, he merely took a hatchet to any offending bulge and got rid of it. It was so simple – and rapid.

The ceiling too, possessed novel and downright fascinating points of interest. For example, it was not all of the same height. Indeed, one part of it, the central component, was several inches lower than all the rest. Horatio put this down initially to what he called lamentably poor workmanship (his actual words were slightly stronger than this) in a very old stained glass window that he had found.

This amazing window had been 'rescued' from an empty chapel which was up for sale. The picture in the stained glass was of 'Jesus Walking on the Waters', which seemed to Horatio to be a perfect metaphor for his own unique gifts to the world of architecture. Sometimes he felt he could walk on water too.

Being very old and designed for mounting vertically, the window proved to be an issue. Its sudden exposure to the almost horizontal meant that the slender lead strips holding the glass in place had sagged severely and even threatened to fall out. Horatio cured the problem simply and quickly by nailing a sheet of strong, clear polythene beneath it, thus preventing the glass from falling out – or if it did, the sheet would catch it.

'There aren't many conservatories with a stained glass roof, so I'm buggered if I'm taking that one out!' was the reply of a confident and proud man. 'Look at the colours! Bloody marvellous!'

It was just ten days after the final second-hand window and piece of old timber had been nailed into place (rusty, used nails were a real hindrance, most of them having to be straightened out) that the first rain fell.

The results were not reassuring. Several buckets were employed to catch the water that penetrated the structure – but that could be sorted out. Some old cast iron guttering was placed at those points inside where there was most ingress, channelling the water outside through the open door. What he was going to do if the door had to be closed in winter, Gladys failed to understand.

She was sensitive and had always been afraid of being burgled. The thought of having to leave the lean-over door open all night in case of rain sat rather uncomfortably with her. Horatio's solution of sleeping with a baseball bat under his pillow in case of an intruder was not sufficiently reassuring.

Again, he had demonstrated the amazing simplicity with which his creative mind was working. It was one of those rare conservatories that had its rainwater guttering on the inside rather than the outside. What an innovation!

'People don't think things through, see? With the gutters on the inside, I won't need to climb onto the roof of the thing to do repairs (something that was in any case structurally impossible) and I can see where the water's coming in too.' It was yet another logical assertion that was difficult to deny.

The next stage of the project was to install the plumbing and especially a bath. Until that time, the whole family had to use a tin bath in front of the fire: not a satisfactory arrangement with two growing girls in the family. But Horatio had things in hand. He had been gradually stockpiling scrap lengths of copper pipe and the odd tap and was ready to embark upon Stage Two – the water system.

A bath had been found in the nearby river so that presented no problem at all. That its enamel had long given up being smooth was not an issue: 'I'll just paint over the thing. I'll recycle some white paint from somewhere. Tons of it 'anging 'round.'

But having installed neither foundations or drains, he realised the bath would not empty unless he raised the end remote from the plughole and elevated the whole thing above the level of the outside paving – necessitating a further brick under all four feet. Once the water was outside it would be down to nature to take care of, he argued, not realising that his garden sloped towards the house, not away from it.

Having two bricks under the feet at one end of the bath and single bricks under those at the other meant that entry and exit to and from the installation could be a little awkward; but that was a secondary problem that could be solved later. Gladys in particular raised objections to this.

'Well, stand on a bloody chair, woman!' was his characteristically reassuring reply.

To be fair to her, her legs hadn't been too good these days. She was increasingly complaining about having contracted the embarrassing complaint of Heavy Legs.

Heavy Legs was a relatively new illness to Abertwp. She was convinced she had it, after reading the previous week's article in the Abertwp Herald written by its health correspondent. The correspondent was not actually medically qualified, but he did his best. In fact the anonymous advisor on all things medical was Goronwy Davies, the slaughterhouse foreman: a man singularly experienced in all things visceral, even if his learning was all gained from dead sheep.

Unfortunately, the bath taps that Horatio had rescued from the tip were not both of the same type. In fact one was an outside or garden tap and the other was a stopcock; but that did not deter him from realising his objective.

The outside tap he augmented with several additional fittings so that it would eventually connect to a suitable copper pipe which he was certain to 'liberate' from somewhere soon. He was a great believer in having faith – something would always turn up, even copper pipe. He did, however, admit to himself that the addition of so many extra brass fittings ('adaptions', he called them) had made the garden tap extremely heavy. In fact, he reckoned that the complex assembly would need supporting. But he didn't want to cross his bridges before his eggs had hatched and would sort that out later.

The stopcock was much more challenging: it had clearly been installed for many decades in an old house somewhere and was almost impossible to turn. Whoever 'liberated' the stopcock had not bothered to free it from its lead piping but had just cut the pipes either side of it, which were still firmly soldered into the brass body of the seized-up device.

He admitted secretly that this had him baffled at first. Either he had to remove both pieces of lead piping by heating the stopcock (but then he didn't know how he would connect the wished-for, hoped-for copper piping to it); or, and this was his preferred option, he would have to find a way of connecting the (wished-for, hoped-for) copper pipe to one side of the thing whilst beating out the lead on the other side into a shape that resembled a spout. Such a direct and simple solution was nothing short of plumbing genius (he claimed).

The latter solution he was quick to execute: a few blows with his faithful coal hammer from the coalhouse changed the shape of the lead immediately – in fact rather significantly so, so that the end of the lead pipe was now almost completely flattened and therefore blocked. It was a shape not exactly as he'd envisaged, but he argued that the water would find a way out somehow, probably in the form of a few jets, or with a bit of luck, a spray.

'All bathrooms 'ave showers now – this'll be ours.'

But he could not avoid having to face up to joining the remaining lead pipe on the other side of the stopcock to a length of copper pipe. He couldn't rely on the coal hammer to help him solve that problem.

One day, he was rummaging around in the back of Geraint Jones' ironmonger's shop (actually 'Jones' Emporium – Suppliers to the Gentry of all Things Sanitary'), when he spotted something entirely new – Super Glue.

He had never seen this before and according to the write-up on the packet, it 'glues everything, from glass to ceramics, from copper to lead'. The latter description stood out like the light outside the Bomb and Dagger on a dark night: it would do precisely what he wanted – join copper to lead! He left Jones'

Emporium (Suppliers to the Gentry of all Things Sanitary) with his new, super solution to an old problem.

'Modern science eh? Bloody marvellous!'

Then, as sometimes happens, Lady Luck smiled on him even more brightly. One of his Buffalo friends called at the house and gave him a length of brand new copper piping that was left over from some work he had been doing on his own house.

He was elated, a condition much feared in the Evans household. That evening, he celebrated generously at the Bomb and Dagger. His fellow celebrants, always keen to know the latest developments in the construction of his lean-over, were treated to a robust description of his latest round of inventiveness, which had been enhanced by the gift of precious copper pipe by one of his mates – who was now drinking more than his fill of Felinfoel's best bitter (from Llanelli, of course). And, innovation of innovations, he'd found Super Glue.

Strange to say, Horatio was surprisingly challenged by the unexpected gift of copper pipe. One thing he could not abide was waste – he saw enough of it every day. This philosophy, admirable though it may have been, was to be severely tested by this length of pipe. This beautiful object of shiny, virginal copper was about four feet long. How was he to use it without cutting it and creating waste?

The answer resulted in an installation that once seen was never forgotten – he refused to cut it at all and used all four feet of it so that it stuck out of the wall by its full length and reached way beyond the centre point of the (sloping) bath.

'I've never wasted such beautiful stuff before and I'm not starting now. Cutting this stuff is a crime. Some poor proletariat sod made this and I am not going to insult him by cutting it up.'

But he didn't mind cutting off some of the short length of lead pipe from the stopcock and gluing into place a short, rather dirty, six-inch length of copper pipe. The gluing operation went so smoothly and so quickly it was a pleasure, although the first two fingers of his left hand took some prising apart.

So the stopcock was almost ready for installation. He managed to fix it to the wall by cementing it in place. This simple solution also meant, he realised, that if the glued joint failed, it would be held together inside the wall. It did, however, mean that the tap was almost an integral part of the wall, making operating it rather difficult. More importantly, being in the wall, rather than over the bath, the spout was not now long enough to direct water into it.

The addition of a chute of bent zinc beneath the tap solved this problem straight away, creating a hoped-for waterfall – a design that has only just been developed in the last decade, which shows conclusively how much in advance of his time he really was.

The hot water tap, with all its heavy brass 'adaptions,' was easily attached to the end of the length of new copper pipe, directing its water (when once it worked) well beyond the centre of the bath.

Whilst this would certainly enable a user to add water to the bath, it made it extremely difficult to enter the bath afterwards. The bather would have to ease themselves under the long pipe with its tap and complex array of adaptions, situated roughly over the navel of most bathers, and then try to avoid them whilst washing.

When one realises that it was impossible to support either the tap or the long pipe it meant that when the tap was turned on, the jet of water would lift the installation, spraying in various directions as it bobbed up and down. On turning off the tap, it would also bob up and down for some time until coming to rest in a gentle arc determined by the mathematics of the laws of gravity and mechanical inertia.

Horatio decided to ignore these theoretical issues and focus on his primary objective: that of having water coming out of taps. He was not going to worry about the pathetic arguments advanced by the females in the family that it would be unpleasant, perhaps even impossible, to use.

But before the bath could be used, it needed hot as well as cold water. The solution was found at the back of the bus station, where some generous, altruistic person had dumped a cracked, cast iron wood-burning stove with one leg missing (the stove, not the person). Fitting a tank for water that could be warmed by the stove's heat would provide the hot water required. Simple.

But where to put the stove? It may seem odd, but the centre of the garden was chosen as the 'obvious' place for it. Away from the delicate structure of the lean-over, its chimney would carry fumes away from the house. A brick or two under the missing leg would sort that out, and it would not be too far from the fuel supply, which was to be coal. Wood, he argued, would not last long enough and there were 'tons of bloody coal under Abertwp' – although his scheme for mining it was not much advanced at this time.

'See? What people don't know is that coal is just very old wood, so a wood stove and a coal stove are the same. 'Course, the bloody capitalists don't tell us that so we buy both. Makes me mad, that!'

Thus it was that Horatio attached a steel tank (once a car's petrol tank rescued from the Cwmtwrch Garage) to the rear of the wood-burning (now coal-burning) stove and got himself a hot water system. But another problem had to be solved: how to get the water to circulate through the stove's water tank?

Rigging an electric flex from the light in the living room (the lean-over had not been equipped with electricity at that time) to a recently 'liberated' central heating pump, suspiciously still in its box and discovered at the back of Jones' Emporium, solved the problem perfectly.

The stove's chimney was a bit of a challenge, but a length of bendy, corrugated aluminium air conditioning trunking sorted that out, supported by no fewer than five bean sticks. 'Can't be too careful with 'eat,' he said. And so the bath was ready for testing. The fire was lit (with wood to begin and then coal) and the circulating pump switched on.

Once the neighbourhood had cleared of smoke (the fire station was in the next street and much anxiety was aroused within, but no-one had called for their help), much gurgling and banging could be heard from the apparatus; but gradually, over the space of an hour or two, the car's petrol tank full of water became warm.

The pendulous tap over the bath, on its long length of new, bendy copper pipe began behaving rather strangely. As the apparatus became warmer, the expected gurgling noises as the water tank became hot, became louder and more alarming. The unsupported and very heavy tap was seen to be moving up and down to the rhythm of the gurgling and rumblings and describing a quite alarming vertical arc on its four-foot length of pipe, until it threatened to hit the base of the bath.

Ever resourceful, Horatio tied up the tap and long pipe to the stained class window in the ceiling with string.

'See? 'Avin wood windows on the roof means I can stick a bloody nail into 'em. Can't do that with fancy aluminium windows!' The tap, its adaptions and the pipe suddenly appeared more sound, less temporary, perhaps. String can do that, if used properly.

The gurgling and rumblings having reached a pitch, Horatio decided it was time to fill the bath with hot, fresh, cleansing water. He'd worked hard and a bath was just what was called for.

The taps were turned on…

What emerged from the hot one surprised everyone: it was a very dark brown, the colour of well-stewed tea, carrying with it deposits of dirt and rust that spread out on the bottom of the bath and splashed over the 'bathroom', as the tap, its adaptions and its long pipe broke loose from the string and oscillated up and down threateningly.

The old stopcock which was supplying cold water down its chute, suddenly decided it didn't want to do that anymore and shot out from the wall, separating from its glued joint and landing at the other end of the bath. No-one was concerned that it may have marked the bath's enamel because there wasn't any. But the jet of high pressure cold water from the fractured pipe within the wall was now hitting the far end of the bath and splashing everywhere.

It was a source of some puzzlement that the floor of the lean-over was also getting very wet, but not from the splashes from the ruptured cold water pipe – the water was coming from outside. The drain on the sloping bath had worked quite well but the garden was refusing to soak up the water and was insisting it flow towards the house.

Meanwhile, out in the centre of the garden where the stove and makeshift boiler were shaking and smoking, surprising things were also happening. Firstly, the bean sticks were alight. They had given up on the improvised, hot chimney, which was melting and had drooped like a wilted flower, spewing noxious smoke onto the garden at low level like a vacuum cleaner in reverse. What Horatio had thought was aluminium was in fact plastic – and was on fire.

Secondly, as the hot water left the system through the oscillating tap, cold water entered the tank back at the boiler to replace it. It seems the plumbing was not prepared for this, and it began to creak and groan as it received the sudden shock of cold water. The noise grew louder and suddenly turned into a booming sound as the cold water behind the stove stirred up some residual petrol that expanded explosively and made its way down the pipe and out through the hot water tap at high pressure.

Even Horatio was not prepared for what happened next: the petrol fumes caught fire from Gladys' Woodbine and the family were treated to the very unusual sight of both water and flames issuing from a tap, which snaked about like a wild animal. It was as though the water itself was on fire, the tap's dragon-like oscillations distributing fire and water everywhere, including onto Gladys, whose apron was badly singed.

Her Woodbine had been extinguished and re-lit twice in the space of a few seconds.

The family stood in stunned silence. Gladys had one of her 'turns' and retreated to the relative safety of the living room where a large supply of tablets and potions were available to treat her conditions. The thought of once again nipping next door for a whiff of Neville's Oxygen bottle resurfaced.

Fresh Woodbines were drawn by her trembling hands out of her apron pocket but failed to calm her nerves. Slouched in one corner of the settee, she was heard to emit a mixture of high-pitched, hysterical whimpers, rather like those of a distressed puppy, accompanied simultaneously by the deep bronchial coughs of a miner: a feat of which many a ventriloquist would be proud.

The girls meanwhile, moved outside into the back garden to avoid the flaming water tap, but immediately realised they were then close to the thundering, overheating stove and its improvised petrol tank boiler. They ran through the house and sought refuge with friends nearby, not sure whether the situation was funny or grave. If the truth were told, they were not only shocked but angry that their dream of a bathroom in a pleasant glass conservatory had ended like this.

But Horatio was up to the challenge. Initially he tried to turn off the flaming tap, but having burned his fingers he grabbed a tea-towel and tried again. Unfortunately, the heat had hardened the washer in the tap and it refused to close. There was nothing for it but to halt the flow of the mixture at the boiler. This too was fraught with difficulties because, wishing to economise on parts, he hadn't equipped it with a stopcock.

Bravery is one feature of leaders and Horatio possessed it in spades; or perhaps he was simply unaware of the dangers. Either way, he strode into the garden and with his trusty coalhouse hammer struck a blow on the outlet pipe which, being constructed Lego-like of many short, miscellaneous lengths of pipe, roughly soldered together, parted immediately.

Jumping back from the flames and hot water, he fell into a row of runner beans, ending in the middle of the structure, with plants and beans draped over his face. He had an amazed look; his eyebrows had reached the highest point on his face, making his eyes bulge like bloodshot beacons.

'Sod it! It wasn't meant to be like this,' he thought secretly to himself. But as he emerged from the runner beans and re-entered the house, his confident smile reasserted itself.

'Just a temp'ry setback, bach,' he told the gasping Gladys, 'just temp'ry.'

She wasn't sure whether to be consoled by this or terrified, because it could mean that he hadn't given up, and his struggle against reality could begin all over again another day.

The family resumed bathing in the tin bath next day and washing in the kitchen sink – once they'd cleared away the debris of plumbing, bricklaying and a thick layer of dust.

As an extra safety measure the girls propped up the lean-over roof with three lengths of wood because the heavy if elegant Edwardian sash windows and the chapel's stained glass window had begun their slow descent. Their weight was clearly in excess of that which Horatio had painstakingly and carefully calculated for the fragile roof structure, made mostly out of orange and tomato boxes.

The chapel's 'Jesus Walking on the Waters' was certainly not as miraculously watertight as he'd thought. As a result, rain entered freely and the water level on the floor rose alarmingly when it rained, in spite of the innovative inner guttering. But it was a problem which he solved easily by stopping up any yawning gaps in the windows with expanding foam – another triumph of science.

Horatio was a master of improvisation; the problem was that his solutions rarely lasted longer than a day or so. Eventually, some two weeks later, Horatio considered the installation complete and fully commissioned.

The installation of electricity is a story all its own, but suffice to say that although his knowledge of electricity was rudimentary, once finished, an electric bulb did glow dimly in the lean-over; although Horatio felt he should issue a safety warning, that no-one should switch it on if they had wet hands or feet. He preferred, he said, that the old, Victorian china and brass switch he'd found ('Beautifully made them was, best you could get when they came out') was best operated by means of either rubber gloves or a wooden pole – both needing to be dry.

But the family wouldn't use the bath after all because he refused to dismantle the pendant tap on its long length of piping, which meant that entry to the high and sloping bath was almost impossible unless the user were able to bend double and twist around at the same time under the four-foot pipe and its heavy brass tap adaptions. The problem of drainage was still unsolved. Why the garden refused to soak up the bath water he found rather annoying.

'The bloody stuff sucks up rain alright, why not bath water?' he asked one of the Brethren, who hadn't a clue, he said. 'Perhaps that's why they do 'ave drains?' the Brother queried.

His decision to preserve the gift of the new pipe intact showed that his appreciation of beautiful plumbing materials was highly developed and his sympathy with the downtrodden member of the proletariat who made it was solid.

'Some poor sod of a worker made that bloody thing, workin' under the cruel lash of a bloodthirsty capitalise. I'm not spoiling 'is workmanship now.'

The girls meanwhile agreed unanimously that the new lean-over was not a success, sagging as it was in the centre and of a rather rhombic shape overall, with yawning holes penetrating its walls. It seemed very different to the conservatory of their dreams and still left much to be desired in terms of water management. They realised they would have to wait a long time until they could luxuriate in a bath whilst looking at the stars through a clear glass roof – even with 'Jesus Walking on the Waters' to reassure them.

To be fair to him, Horatio accepted that further detailed planning (and scavenging for parts) would be required if the project was to be a total success; notably, he must find a hot water boiler that had not seen petrol in its entire life. And perhaps find a more elegant solution to adjusting the slope of the bath than using bricks. A drain would have been handy too.

The talk amongst the communist Brethren and his fellow Buffaloes was that he had managed to construct something which Abertwp had never seen before, but which at any moment could either explode or collapse. But such was Horatio's force of character that no-one dared express any doubts about the integrity of the installation – at least, to his face.

Behind his back, expressions of amusement were rife. To make things worse, Gladys and the two girls had been offered the liberal use of next doors' bathrooms by both their neighbours, out of sheer pity. The shame of seeing them leaving the new installation unused hurt Horatio deeply. He was at a loss to understand why his amazing DIY skills had failed to charm his family.

To him, this edifice, costing nothing and rising out of the ground uniquely as a result of his inventiveness and keen observation for discarded items, (finding 'Jesus Walking on the Waters' was a master stroke) would have defeated a lesser man.

The Wardrobe

Number 74, Slaughterhouse Terrace was not a large property; in fact it was a very small one. It had only two bedrooms and neither had fitted cupboards of any kind, so that free-standing furniture was needed to store clothes. Two growing girls sharing the same bedroom meant they had an equally growing collection of clothes; but wardrobe there was none.

Until, that is, Horatio spotted one.

It was standing forlornly in the rain at the rear of the Bomb and Dagger. The ash cart halted with a sudden jerk as Horatio's eyes lit up with the discovery that here was a prize worth having: a wardrobe for his girls. This admirable, if not touching sentiment, he nurtured all day, tainted however by the fear that 'some other bugger' might steal it.

But he had a plan: one of the lads would have to hang about and guard it, until they had finished their round and the lorry had dumped its load on the council tip. Then, the desirable bedroom article could be transported to 74 Slaughterhouse Terrace. Simple!

The smallest of the three-man team on the Mk IV ash cart was Terry, a wiry little chap of 23. He was not one of Abertwp's brightest voters, but he was good at taking orders, even if, as frequently occurred, he didn't understand them. He was faintly aware of this intellectual weakness, but it was more than offset by being a close associate, nay a devoted follower, of his hero Horatio Evans. It should not be thought Terry worshipped him, but it was as close to hero worship as it was possible to get in a town like Abertwp.

And so it was that as the ash cart left the scene, he was left alone with the wardrobe. It was quiet in the back lane and the rain fell steadily. It took Terry quite a while to realise he was not enjoying himself. Standing there alone in the rain, unable to even light a Woodbine, he had a flash of inspiration and decided he could do his sentry duty just as well inside the wardrobe as outside it.

'Why get wet, after all?' he suddenly realised.

This is how Terry (the son of a funeral director's assistant in the embalming department, and an immigrant from distant England) responded to most things in life: it took quite a while for things to sink in, but when they did the solution came like a flash. In fact his nickname amongst the ash cart fraternity was Flash. Sad to say he didn't realise why: he thought his colleagues were comparing him to the then popular Flash Gordon, the cinematic hero, or were subtly implying that he was mentally quick. The use of double irony and the power of the double entendre were as yet unknowns to Terry. He preferred to believe he was mentally 'quick', the definition of which, was uniquely his own.

The key to the wardrobe was missing, but the doors opened easily and in he slipped. Sliding to the bottom of one side of the piece of furniture, with his knees bent double, he was quite comfortable, although smoking his Woodbines in such a tight, enclosed space was using up so much Oxygen that within the hour he was asleep.

Luckily for him, no-one else seemed to want the wardrobe so he wasn't disturbed. A further stroke of luck was that the ash cart finished its round, in spite of being one man down, in record-breaking time. The effect on the streets of Abertwp could be seen by the keen-eyed voter to have resulted in numerous dustbins remaining un-emptied. The Mk IV was capable of a fair turn of speed, an asset employed to the full in completing that day's round. (It was estimated by a retired traffic policeman that the Horatio Express had driven through the narrow lanes of the town at speeds in excess of 50mph in places.)

The shift over, the Mk IV returned to the rear of the pub. The wardrobe stood exactly where they had left it, albeit now rhombic in shape, being tilted to one side under Terry's weight, and emitting Woodbine smoke.

On opening the doors they found him puffing away on his last one and looking decidedly green. Carbon monoxide poisoning, it is said, is not a pleasant way to go. But Woodbine poisoning was an entirely new phenomenon and Terry was definitely showing its symptoms: the principle of which, besides a deep-seated cough, was a stupid grin on his face and an inability to realise where he was (although they weren't sure if that was actually a symptom or exaggerated normality). When told he was in a wardrobe he simply laughed, which must have been a secondary symptom of Woodbine poisoning.

He had to be brought round and there was nothing for it but to appeal to the good offices of Geraint the pub landlord in serving Terry (and why not the others?) a pint or two of his diluted brew. It seemed to do the trick and all three men were then ready for the final stage of the project, to transport the wardrobe to number 74, Slaughterhouse Terrace. It was done remarkably quickly, although numerous scratches in the item's delicate French polished body had appeared.

'You won't notice those after a while,' boasted Horatio, 'after all, it's about a 'undred bloody years old, what can you expect from antiques? It's called 'patina', lads, in the trade, that's what it is, patina,' he announced confidently and confidentially as though imparting a Masonic secret of the antiques trade.

Thus it was that poor Gladys, although having a bad day from her multiple ailments, almost dropped to the ground when the three lads appeared at the front door with their new-found gift.

Collapsing onto the settee, she prayed aloud in Welsh to the good Lord to help her, as another Woodbine was shakily lit up and she began whimpering quietly. Horatio's surprises (she called them shocks) had happened so often that she knew with a certainty verging on perfect clairvoyance that it would end badly. She was even thinking of popping next door to have another whiff of Neville's Oxygen bottle to 'help her chest', as she put it. Her asthma pump and two Valium tablets did help a little.

'I need morphine, I do, not bloody Valium. The pain, the pain… oh, God 'elp me; what's 'e brought in yer now?' was the sad refrain from the suffering Gladys, seeing her tiny home once again threatened by its lord and master's initiatives. It was actually a pity she didn't pop next door. The next hour or two were to be 'interesting' to say the least. Perhaps we ought to say dramatic.

Miners' cottages from the 19th century were not built for tall people, nor did they have much of a hallway. Basically, the front door opened into the living room, except for a space just big enough to open the door and perhaps accommodate someone squeezing their way out. The wardrobe, however, had been built for a grander homestead with taller ceilings and it was not going out, it was coming in.

It must be said, in his defence, that Horatio managed what Terry reckoned was impossible: the wardrobe was tilted and tipped, twisted and turned and eventually there it stood, in the living room, more or less upright. It was not, however, in one piece. Regrettably, it had been essential that the ornate (they thought ugly) carved headpiece atop the wardrobe be removed. None of them liked it and they were men of some discernment in these things. The rusty coalhouse hammer removed it rapidly and painlessly with only minimal tearing of the veneer on the front.

They all agreed it looked an imposing piece. So imposing in fact that no-one moved – they couldn't, due to its size. Iolo (a sensitive and secretive harmonica player in his spare time) reckoned its volume to be roughly a third of that of the entire room. Even without its Victorian headpiece, it almost touched the ceiling boards between the exposed beams of the cottage. So in order to move it at all, it had to be repeatedly tilted and shoved beneath one beam after another and only allowed to assume an upright position once it was standing between any two of the beams.

These manoeuvres demanded not only strength and teamwork but space. Space, however, was not a plentiful commodity at number 74. The settee on which Gladys had collapsed was taking up quite a bit of the precious stuff and was therefore unceremoniously lifted into the air and moved into the back garden with Gladys still on it.

Her otherwise quiet whimpering moved up an octave and increased in volume by multiple decibels until they became screams. The two girls ran to pacify her, both of them accompanying her in Welsh prayers, knowing that they usually helped her calm down.

Meanwhile indoors, the desirable antique with its valuable patina (or deep gouges) was standing at the foot of the stairs, its dark menacing presence creating an atmosphere of doom in the room – as though a couple of very large, threatening policemen had walked in and wouldn't be moved. It was indeed intimidating. Its huge bulk darkened the room, made even more sombre by its deep mahogany veneer – what was left of it.

It seemed as though Horatio was to be defeated. The stairs in such cottages are not straight; to save space they are steep, narrow and have a very sharp bend.

Iolo began to edge towards the door, because he was a little upset. He had been able to see Gladys through the open back door in a state of total collapse (sensitive harmonica players are like that). Terry too was uneasy, but was (typically) mystified as to why. To their relief, Horatio dismissed them both!

'Right lads, thanks for yer 'elp today, I'll sort out the rest. You can bugger off if you like.'

With no idea how he was to lift the thing up the steep, narrow stairs, both Horatio's associates were more than glad to go home. The two of them escaped what they imagined would be a titanic struggle that could be awful to watch.

The wardrobe faced Horatio at his most determined.

Gladys, meanwhile, who was still outside in the garden, had managed to stand, breathing in deeply to 'help her chest' and asked one of the girls to go to the shop to replenish her stock of Woodbines – 'get forty, love, I needs 'em.' It seemed her prayers and appeals to Heaven may have begun to work. She felt a little better for being away from Horatio and out in the fresh air.

She and the girls, all three sitting on the settee next to the carrots, eventually realised that things were eerily quiet in the house, which was not only odd, but worrying. They poked their heads around the doorway and were puzzled at what they saw: Horatio was doing nothing.

He walked (squeezed) around the wardrobe, as best he was able, sizing up the problem, literally. Gladys had to admit that although Horatio's constant 'innovations' as he called them, drove her to distraction, seeing him doing nothing like this was completely unnerving. It was like waiting for a clap of thunder that never comes.

'For God's sake don't just stand there, do something, you're making me scared,' was the only thing she could say, followed by several bronchial convulsions.

'Listen now, Luv, it's no good rushin' into things and making mistakes. Too many people does that,' he replied. It was a statement that should have been cast in brass, polished and erected over the mantelpiece.

'Good God he's bloody mad!' were the last words heard from Gladys as she grabbed the door frame and slipped onto a kitchen chair.

The power of silence is an amazing thing, Horatio noted.

Not believing in the arithmetical limitations inevitably imposed by actually measuring the size of the wardrobe, he called into play his amazing gift of estimating accurately three-dimensional space. (Dustmen are good at this.) And he came quickly to the conclusion that 'it wasn't going to go.' He didn't, however, vocalise this conclusion, even though the two girls, Gladys and the two other members of the Mk IV in-cart crew had already made the same observation – to themselves.

Leaders are often assailed by the many doubts of their followers and have to learn not to listen to them. What Gladys and the girls were therefore witnessing was a leader in deep thought, weighing up the pros and cons, not being rushed into precipitous action. Either that or he was stumped.

Finally, he left the room with slow, measured, assured steps and made his way down the garden to his shed. This amazing construction had remained more or less upright for years, even though it had a distinct and, in the opinion of Horatio, a 'slight list' to starboard. It was known as the Leaning Shed of Pisa.

One of the effects of its inherent angle of inclination, was the difficulty opening the door, which would strike the ground. The rest of the family had no desire whatsoever to enter it (considering it too dangerous) so there was no risk of anyone taking anything of value – the most valuable item in it was a shovel he had 'liberated' from British Rail.

He disappeared into the depths of this peculiar tilting edifice and emerged with a large saw, at the sight of which Gladys had another 'turn'. She decided the only place she was safe was in the outside loo, which was another interesting construction, but one that had stood for many years, being built by Victorian bricklayers. It was a place in which the occupant felt fairly safe. To be quite sure of her safety, and now well supplied with Woodbines, she bolted the door.

Although Horatio didn't like smoking, the sight of Gladys' smoke leaking lazily out through the several v-shaped cuts in the top of the door was somewhat poetic, he thought. It reminded him of a painting he'd once seen of a lonely mountain farmstead with smoke rising lazily from its chimney as the sun set. He'd always felt that the smoke in the painting implied that a contented state of family bliss reigned within. In the same way, he liked to see Gladys' smoke rising lazily from the brick privy, his interpretation being that Gladys was (reasonably) content and her bowels were working well.

Horatio took the saw inside and looked once more at the dark, menacing presence of the wardrobe. He had a plan. If its height was a problem, he'd reduce it. He noticed it had four legs and these had to go. A few energetic cuts with the saw solved the problem, although not very neatly or evenly. The result was a leaning wardrobe: one that leant forwards as though admonishing the observer.

'These things'll burn well,' he thought, turning the legs over in his hands. 'Not needed though these days. Don't need legs no more.'

But the sheer bulk of the piece was still problematical. The stairs were clearly far too narrow, too steep and had far too tight a bend in them to accept such a thing.

'Removin' the doors 'll lighten it,' he thought, 'an then it'll be easier to 'andle.'

Off they came (he actually used a screwdriver this time,

although the screws were allowed to bounce around the room and were lost under various items of furniture) and both doors were parked against the sideboard.

Now his true genius shone through. Taking the saw, he began cutting the wardrobe in two – vertically of course. The first cut did, unfortunately, remove more of the French-polished veneer from the front, but 'needs must'. Besides, his army experience had taught him that under fire, most initiatives can result in collateral damage, and this one was no exception.

Cutting through the thick top, the saw reached the back of the wardrobe and quickly descended to its base through the paper-thin backboard. A final effort brought the saw to the front as it finally cut through the base. To the experienced eye, the saw-cuts thus produced were not actually straight: in fact they were, frankly, very jagged, which would make the reuniting of the subsequent two halves rather tricky. But that test of his craftsmanship in wood would come later.

This is where Terry and Iolo would have come in handy, because the two halves then parted company and fell away from each other, one hitting the floor with a crash, the other striking the sideboard and sliding across one of the doors, making a deep gouge across it.

Thinking about it later, Horatio realised that it would have been better if two people could have held the halves together right up to the very last saw cut, thus avoiding what actually happened. As the sections said goodbye to each other at the top, they hadn't yet said goodbye to each other at the bottom. But gravity will have its way. They were still both attached to the base, which was struggling now to maintain its integrity against the increasing forces trying to split it.

With his saw still working (uselessly) away, he was taken by surprise as the base suddenly splintered with a sickening bang and a tearing noise rather like veneer being ripped off. He completely ignored these finer issues and continued to focus on the objective: getting the thing upstairs.

No-one could have anticipated his next move. He stood one of the halves upright and suddenly threw his arms around it, hugging it tenderly but firmly as though in a lover's passionate embrace. In this state of amorous determination, he backed towards the stairs and fell backwards as one foot struck the bottom stair and the half-wardrobe fell on him. But this was part of the plan. In such a supine position, his 'darling' of a half-wardrobe in his arms, he was able to inch up the stairs, one at a time, one buttock at a time, pushing with his feet.

His labours took some time and once at the top, the transition from being on his back on the stairs, to being vertical on his feet was not an easy one. At the summit, he realised he was lying on the floor with half a wardrobe pinning him to the linoleum. Like a disenchanted lover he pushed the half-wardrobe off him and rose like a phoenix from beneath it.

His efforts were rewarded and the girls' bedroom saw for the first time half a wardrobe. And it wasn't too tall either, although there was not enough headroom to stand it up without manoeuvring it so that it stood between the ceiling beams.

However, his success was short-lived, as the half-wardrobe was not stable without its other half. It began to twist and threatened to collapse. But he was the master of the situation and placed it face-down (if it could be said to have a face) on the floor awaiting its partner. This too was raised up the stairs in the same lovers' embrace, buttock by buttock. (His bum was sore for days afterwards.)

Both halves were eventually reunited in the same room, but they were not joined in matrimony yet. With the help of the girls who temporarily and rather nervously held the two halves together for him, he quickly descended the stairs and from his wonky shed of Pisa brought a hammer, nails and some bits of tomato boxes that had been stored there for many years and were so old they were grey.

By nailing these pieces of boxwood across the back, the two halves of the wardrobe were eventually re-united, although they weren't a perfect match and it has to be said that the strips of tomato box looked rather untidy; more so when he nailed a few to the top of the wardrobe. It was a pity he used such large nails too, because most of them appeared inside the wardrobe. The ripped and torn base also caused a bit of a problem until he nailed down more tomato boxes to hide the damage.

'Who's going to look round the back or inside?' he said, philosophically. One of the girls almost replied to the question, but instinct kicked in and she stopped.

His attempt to reattach the doors required all his ingenuity. Since the two halves never quite mated again, the doors didn't match properly either. In fact, he had to leave one door off, deciding that modern furniture often had open shelves in it and with some scrap wood (also from the Pisa shed) shelves could easily be installed. One of the girls was heard to whisper: 'If he thinks I'm storing my knickers on dirty tomato boxes, he's got another thing coming.'

So it was that for the first time the girls had a wardrobe, and a wardrobe unlike any other. Sometimes leaders have to overcome practical as well as theoretical difficulties and this time Horatio amply demonstrated he was master of both.

Gladys was too poorly to climb the stairs to look at it immediately. In fact it wasn't until the next day that she was helped up the stairs to witness the dark, brooding presence that had been installed in the girls' bedroom, leaning menacingly away from the wall. One of the girls had already tried pushing some folded cardboard under the front to try and persuade it into the vertical but it was just too heavy.

Gladys queried the safety issues on behalf of the girls (rusty nails sticking out, the strange angle of inclination of the thing and the danger of opening its door) and was assured by Horatio that providing the door was never opened fully, especially when empty, the wardrobe would remain more or less vertical; adding that it was always wise for two people to be present for safety's sake.

Having to have both girls present to open the door was rather annoying, but health and safety considerations are paramount in such things. They did, however, wish their father hadn't nailed a notice on the door instructing the user in how to open the door safely. Being a councillor and an amateur lawyer, he had phrased the notice in legalese that was startling. It was quite some weeks before the girls either tried to open the door, or put anything in it.

The spare door, meanwhile, was destined for other things as we shall see. 'Waste not, want not,' was Horatio's motto as he smiled contentedly at the gift of a wardrobe for the daughters he loved so much.

The Fireplace

I‍T IS EVERY Welshman's pride to come home and see his family warmed before a glowing fire of Welsh anthracite coal. Indeed, for some years Horatio had been able to satisfy himself on this precise achievement, although the anthracite was somewhat suspect. It wasn't supposed to smoke, but his did. But he still swore it was anthracite.

But satisfaction with a domestic fire derives from more than just the coal that burns in it; its surroundings, namely the fireplace, contribute too. A drab, utilitarian fireplace detracts from the pride in having such a fire. And so it was that Gladys was occasionally dissatisfied by hers.

The driver of a Mk IV is in an enviable position, both physically and economically. From high up in his cab, he surveys at a glance the detritus of others, whilst creating economic opportunities for himself. As he once put it:

'I don't call it rubbish, I calls it gifts.'

So it was, that one Friday morning in November, our keen-eyed 'gift collector' spotted something that shouted out to be saved – an abandoned fireplace.

'Just what she'd like,' he said to himself, 'she' being Gladys of course.

He also repeated his observation to Iolo and Terry who recognised immediately the potential for getting involved in another dangerous 'project' that their beloved captain was plotting.

Having experienced, during the wardrobe raid, their ability

to drive around the streets of Abertwp at high speed and leave enough time to collect such gifts and take them home before the end of their shift, the plucky trio repeated the same tactic. True, as before, much remained uncollected, but surely a few voters here and there could wait a week for the boys' next round of the town? Especially if the crew made sure that the rubbish of those voters in positions of authority was collected as usual.

Like wardrobes, fireplaces are not easy things to handle. They are not only heavy, but if tiled (and they usually are), they are fragile. Ash carts, even the Mk IV, are, for some reason, not well designed for lifting or transporting fireplaces, a design fault that Horatio bemoaned. But the gift this time was in a pretty good position, on open waste ground behind the toilet bowl factory (motto: 'Flushed With Success'). The Mk IV had plenty of space in which to manoeuvre.

Additionally, the fireplace was leaning almost upright against a wall, beneath some trees. In a flash, Horatio realised he was in luck. Being already upright, it would be a doddle to pass some rope around its middle and hoist it in the air using the branch of one of the trees. Reversing the ash cart beneath the suspended gift would provide a straightforward method of loading it onto the vehicle.

Simplicity is the mark of genius.

Iolo got some rope and slipped it around the middle of the fireplace. Meanwhile, Terry climbed the tree and was waiting to catch the rope as it was thrown to him. Almost immediately (which was most unusual for him), Terry realised that the coefficient of friction between the rope and the branch was too high to allow the fireplace to be hoisted. (Actually, he didn't mention the coefficient of friction, but used a few choice words that meant the same thing – 'it's stuck' was his considered conclusion.)

Horatio was not to be beaten. 'Of course it's not going to slip around the branch, idiot! But we'll use some grease so it does,' moaned Horatio, looking skyward.

He nipped back to the Mk IV and brought out another gift, a tin of grease that had been hanging around unloved and unwanted outside the Upper Cwmtwrch Garage. The garage was renowned for its highly decorated breakdown lorry that had the owner's philosophy of life emblazoned across its front and sides:

'23½ hour breakdown service (we needs a break)'
'In God we trust, the rest pays cash'.

The grease helped, but it didn't do the whole job. Some lift was obtained, but the rope was still catching on the bark of the tree.

'Teflon's what we need,' shouted Iolo and went to the back of the Horatio Express where he'd noticed a baking tray.

'Bloody ideal, this,' he boasted, as he bent the tray into a curve to go around the branch and to be inserted beneath the greased rope.

'Hey! That's my mam's tray,' cried Terry as he realised what had become of his mother's baking tray, another gift from the voters of Abertwp.

Horatio was much impressed. He and Iolo heaved on the rope and the fireplace began its ascent. Then they hit a snag; they could only lift it about 18 inches at a time with each pull; at that point, they needed to change hands for another pull to raise it more.

They made a mess of their first transition from one pull to the next: Iolo let go his grip and Horatio couldn't hold it. So the fireplace dropped to the ground in a cloud of dust with a number of tiles flying off at its base.

So Terry was told to 'Get down by yer, goo'boy,' as he slipped to the ground.

His job was to wedge something beneath the gift as it rose each time. How to do this was not obvious to him – or even to a man of normal IQ, but noticing a large pile of bricks across the other side of the patch, he busied himself with collecting as many as he could to pile beneath it as it rose, one pull at a time.

The system worked. As Iolo and Horatio hauled on the rope and the gift rose into the air, Terry built up the bricks beneath. The gift was then gently lowered onto them whilst Iolo and Horatio changed hands and they were ready to haul away again.

Now, freestanding bricks, piled one on top of the other are not very stable. Any rough ground on which the first ones are placed won't help either. So quite quickly the two piles began to show a definite deviation from the vertical. In fact, on the fourth lift, the piles were so unstable that Iolo in particular felt distinctly uneasy about the shaky edifice that was rising before him.

'I don't like the look of this bloody thing,' he pointedly grumbled, ''Ow 'igh does it go before it brains us?'

He had a point. The back of the ash cart, the gift's intermediate destination, was at least four feet off the ground. So far, they had managed about two foot six and were worried about losing a couple of toes if the fireplace crashed to the ground.

It is in just such situations, when followers doubt their own abilities and mortal danger seems to threaten, that leaders come into their own. This was no exception. Horatio shouted to Terry to 'Bloody well go and get the cart and reverse it over by yer, quick while we 'olds it!'

His superior powers of deduction had led him to realise that not all the gift need be at a height of four feet from the ground; if most of it was, then gravity and a good heave would help tilt the rest into the back of the cart, albeit upside down.

The vehicle reversed, although rather too rapidly for comfort, Terry not being used to driving it. It backed up against the fireplace, pushing it back a little, and sure enough it tilted the top of it towards the open jaws of the vehicle.

'Now come by yer with us, you twerp, and 'elp us lift the damn thing into the cart, and don't forget to put the brakes on!' urged Horatio (inspirational words from an inspirational leader).

Sure enough, it worked. Although the base of the fireplace was only two feet six inches off the ground, the top was higher than the back of the ash cart. The three of them heaved it into the back with relative ease.

Tiles flew off the top and front with equal ease, and a crack appeared, running most of the height of it as it struck the steel base of the vehicle. But the major bulk of the thing was intact.

'Don't worry boys, dab of Polyfilla works wonders! I can always find some spare tiles later to stick on,' assured their leader.

And off they went to 74 Slaughterhouse Terrace to present their gift to the family. Not only were Gladys and her daughters blissfully unaware of the impending donation, but one of the girls was taking a bath in front of the fire.

Now a Council Mk IV ash cart cannot be kept waiting, especially if it doesn't belong to you. So the girl was turfed out of the tin tub and told to dress in the kitchen 'Whilst me and the boys brings this in.'

Of course Gladys was at a complete loss (again) to understand what on earth Horatio had brought home this time. She was only just beginning to recover from both the wardrobe project and construction of the lean-over. Surely not another 'project'?

'Got something by yer, bach, you'll like. Like new it is. You'll love it. Just rake out the fire will you?'

Gladys was actually pretty sharp, in spite of her illnesses, but the idea of chucking out one of her daughters from her bath, and actually scraping out red hot coals from a living fire onto the hearth, seemed so outside her realm of comprehension that she felt she needed help – from the good Lord above, judging by the Welsh prayer she began reciting in a rising, hysterical voice. Her renowned rendition of 'Bread of Heaven' was supplanted this time by 'On a Green Hill Far Away', which is precisely where she wished she was.

Totally incapable of executing Horatio's order, she just stood wide-eyed, whilst he grabbed the poker and pulled out the red-hot coals onto the hearth.

Dense smoke rose to the ceiling of the small room, making a thick sulphurous cloud out of which Gladys managed to stagger into the kitchen, coughing alarmingly. If they'd had a canary it would have died instantly. Gas was present at 74 Slaughterhouse Terrace.

Smoke was also rising from the mat in front of the hearth and it was burning nicely, having received a number of cinders, some of them red hot.

Horatio, steadfast man that he was, simply opened the windows and doors and declared the zone clear – although the front door was still not visible and even the girls couldn't breathe. The motto over the fireplace – 'God knows what you're doing' – was also totally eclipsed. (Did God really know what Horatio was doing, Gladys wondered?)

The next operation was difficult and dangerous. So much so, that both Terry and Iolo escaped quickly once the gift had been successfully unloaded into the room.

They had brought the fireplace through the front door alright by man-handling it; but from there onwards it needed careful manipulation in the confines of the small living room. They did this with relative ease, in spite of its weight, by sliding it along the spare wardrobe door and the polished central leaf from the dining table – one that was never used because the room wasn't wide enough.

'See? You needs smooth surfaces to slide things along, boys. Can't beat French polish for that. Just look at that wardrobe door. Marvellous and smooth it is. Just right, you watch,' Horatio assured them.

Perhaps his use of the present tense was misjudged, because the surfaces of both the wardrobe door and the dining table leaf were definitely not smooth by the end of the operation. Deep gouges ran across both surfaces.

'Is that more patina, boss?' joked Iolo, smiling.

'Now then, now then, that's enough joking. Sometimes the end justifies the means, boys, justifies the means. Don't forget that, now. (Philosophy was never absent for long from Horatio's mind.) Anyway, thanks boys, you can take the lorry back now – see you after the weekend.'

So now the little living room had two fireplaces: one installed, with the remnants of its fire smoking away in the hearth and burning on the mat; and a new one, with quite a number of tiles missing and a crack down the middle, propped next to it. Without even bothering to remove his coat, Horatio set about the task of swopping them around.

'No time like the present,' he grunted as he wielded the coal hammer and, with a crowbar, prised the old fireplace from the wall. Just in time, one of the girls caught the clock as it slid off the mantelpiece, but failed to catch a figurine of Owain Glyndŵr on horseback which fell, Owain-first, into the pile of burning coal.

Everyone was surprised when Owain began to melt and finally burst into flame. The 'solid brass' figurine (another gift) had clearly not been genuine – but that's the risk one takes when picking up things from the tip.

It was surprising how easily the old fireplace came away from the wall. So easily in fact, that it was fortunate Horatio was able to throw his hammer and crow bar onto the settee in order to catch it as it fell forwards, bringing entire lengths of wallpaper and much of the skirting board with it.

A huge effort on his part saw him dragging the thing one end at a time through the kitchen and letting it fall into a patch of carrots. He'd decided he'd dispense with the wardrobe door and the dining table extension to do this, in order to save time. This wasn't impatience on his part, just showing how focused he was on the objective.

'Anyway,' he argued to himself, 'since I'm chucking this old one out, it don' matter if it gets bashed.' (That it might bash furniture and fittings in the process he had decided to ignore.)

As he demonstrated with the wardrobe, he was not inclined to get confused with detailed measurements, so he hadn't really any idea if the new fireplace would fit. It looked roughly the same size, until he realised that the opening in this new one was definitely smaller than the old one. In fact, it had been a bedroom fireplace. The fire opening would have to be modified.

Coalhouse hammer in hand, he began sculpting the fire brick bit by bit until it looked about the right size. Unfortunately, fire brick is very fragile and the final knock did not do it much good. A crack appeared, not where he'd struck it, but right at the back of the firebrick. Investigating the fissure with his crowbar, (not the best idea, he admitted afterwards) he mistakenly prised the crack open – wide.

To his surprise the crack was still widening of its own accord. Getting onto his knees to see better what was going on, he saw a face staring back at him from within the enlarging fissure. It was Mr Davies from next door.

Some words, which cannot be printed here, were exchanged through this yawning fissure and more afterwards over the front garden wall. They were to the effect that if Horatio didn't sort out what he'd done, Mr Davies ('The Beast of Abertwp' to his cage-fighting friends) would sort him out.

Cool under fire, Horatio returned to the fire grate. Mixing some stale cement left over from building the 'lean-over', adding some fresh Polyfilla for good measure, he sealed the opening in the fire brick. With more heaving and shoving he dragged the new fireplace into place, leaving behind it an interesting set of deep grooves in the linoleum.

True, the new fireplace did have an inch gap between it and the wall, but that could be sorted out with a bit more cement later.

Luckily for him, he was able to complete the repairs to Mr Davies' fireplace the next day because it was a Saturday and he didn't have to go to work.

'Makes you think you should always start a job on a Friday in case it goes wrong,' he mused.

He spent most of the day sealing the gaps between the new fireplace and the wall and stuffing old rope around the inside of the grate to fill the gap between it and the fire brick. He'd seen this done before and thought it a brilliant idea for filling such gaps.

But ordinary rope, such as he used, burns. It was a special heat-proof rope that he must have seen used previously, but this difference only became apparent once he'd re-lit the fire. The rope caught quite quickly, saturated as it was with creosote. This particular gift had been found behind the watchman's hut at the railway sidings and had been soaked in creosote so as not to rot. People on railways do things like that.

The smell of burning hemp and creosote drifted downwind of number 74 and was picked up at the bus stop in front of Gwen's café. Some customers said they felt unwell from the smell and refused to eat even her renowned Welsh Cakes.

Counter-intuitively, Horatio's solution was to close all

the doors and windows and to sit it out until the smoking stopped. Unfortunately, this meant that not only was the house uninhabitable, notably by Gladys who had already caught the bus to her mother's, but once the rope had finished burning (scorching the tiles of the fireplace in the process) it opened up the very gap that it was meant to seal. So what Horatio termed 'natural smoke' (that from the coal) poured into the room.

'I don't mind dirty smoke in its natural form,' he told himself as he sat alone, suffocating in the darkened room, 'but I can't abide unnatural smoke.'

He had obviously classified the smoke from burning Welsh anthracite as 'natural' and therefore OK. That from creosote-soaked British Railways rope was unnatural and not OK.

In spite of having entreated the two girls to stay with him, our hero was left alone for some time and was totally invisible under a dense cloud of choking fumes.

'Years ago I swear we used creosote to clear the chest,' he said to himself, 'a couple of hours in by yer might do Gladys the world of good.'[1]

He had to admit that this had not been one of the easiest of enterprises, but he wasn't really sure what had been wrong with the plan. His aversion to measuring anything had perhaps been a weakness this time.

Hours later, one of the girls ventured back, as much as anything to check that her father was alive. He wasn't there. Frightened, she looked in the back kitchen and into both bedrooms, from one of which she saw him at the top of the garden digging up some late carrots. She went downstairs and into the garden.

She pointed out the foolishness of his enterprise and added

---

[1]   He may have been thinking about coal-tar, not creosote. Coal-tar was used for the treatment of lice, not a cough. It is actually deadly – as is creosote. [Ed.]

a detail about the new fireplace she had noticed: not only was it missing many tiles and had a crack in it, but it was also not as wide as the old one so that the old hearth stuck out on either side of it. As for the missing wallpaper and wrecked skirting boards she didn't even bother mentioning them. The girl did not stay long but returned to her friends, complaining that there was still too much smoke emerging from the gaps in the fireplace.

Somewhat dejected, Horatio nipped out surreptitiously and asked one of the Brethren, a builder, what he could do about it. He didn't admit he had tried stuffing creosote-soaked rope into the gaps, but felt there must be a solution to the problem. He came home with a tin of special heat-proof filler that his mate had given him.

'See? Always ask if you're not sure,' he told himself, 'no good pressing on regardless.'

On his way home he happened to glance down the back lane near Jones' Emporium (Suppliers of Everything Sanitary to the Gentry) and noticed a pair of rather interesting items, just standing there, on their own, obviously lonely.

They were statues of some Greek-like goddesses, holding grapes or something – it was difficult to tell what they were holding. They were about four feet tall and were badly broken, one having an arm missing and the other a foot, making the latter look very tense. In both cases their grapes were, strictly speaking, unidentifiable, but the casual observer, given sufficient alcohol and a degree of Myopia, might assume they were meant to be holding grapes[2].

Thus it was that when Gladys returned from her mother's the next day she entered a living room that was transformed.

---

[2]   It was later established that they were holding bags of powdered Polyfilla. They were plaster statues advertising the product. They had been in the back of Jones' shop for years. [Ed.]

The offending new fireplace was there (leaning outwards); large areas of wallpaper were missing, as was the skirting board; but at either side of the fireplace, standing on the old hearth, were two alabaster nudes advertising a new filler cement.

'I can see you like it, bach! No, don't say it, there's no need to thank me, thank the bloody Council. It was their cart! What a difference, eh?'

The girls said nothing and covered the nudes with tea cloths as soon as their father left for the Buffaloes.

The Kind Kangaroo

I T WAS A Thursday evening and there he was, our hero, leaning on the end of the bar at the Bomb and Dagger chatting to Mavis the barmaid. At least, this is what he thought he was doing. In fact she never said a word and was usually nowhere near him, preferring to keep within her own zone of misery some yards away.

She wasn't a buxom maid; in fact she was a thin, rather sad girl, with a pronounced stoop. She looked as though she had just been released from a week standing in the stocks, her head bowed to avoid missiles. Her head was no longer employed in looking forward, but downward.

Her hair mirrored her mood: it too was 'sad' – lank, thin and, to be frank, rather greasy, the poor girl could depress anyone just by looking at her. Undertakers lowering the latest deceased voter of Abertwp into the earth were hilarious comedians by comparison.

Her dress sense was interesting, consisting of frocks of indeterminate colour and style. They could have been modelled on sacks, hanging from her feeble frame in the simplest of straight lines. Her habit of always wearing Wellington boots (without socks) didn't help either.

She never seemed to see the lighter side of life, which was a distinct handicap for a barmaid. As many a visitor discovered, it was no good passing the time of day with her because she appeared deaf to such niceties, as though completely consumed by some secret grief. For her, the end was not nigh: it had already happened. The idea of engaging in a response was anathema to her. Even a customer's smile was wasted effort, because that would require her to look at them, which she never did.

Why Geraint employed her no-one could understand; but the reason was very simple: Mavis was so off-putting, so depressing, so uncommunicative that no customer was going to bother complaining to her about anything, especially his watered-down beer. Geraint didn't want a good barmaid: he needed suicidal Mavis. She was the most effective barrier to customer dissatisfaction yet devised by man.

But Horatio's caring side was showing and he was trying to improve her mood by explaining the finer points of the Communist revolution to come and how she was a downtrodden serf to a capitalist landlord. He pushed home his points by following her up and down the bar, raising his voice against the background chatter and prodding the air in front of her face. Unfortunately, the more she tried to escape, the more he slid along the sticky counter, glass in hand, and pursued her.

Her depressed mood did not improve and eventually turned to anger.

'Listen, old Geraint might be a right sod, but 'e's never trod on me, never; just let him try! Anyway, why should the likes of you, who always looks as though your face 'as been trodden on good and proper, tell me what's wrong with my life? I bloody well know what's wrong with my life, thank you, and it's got nothing to do with anyone treading on me. So bugger off.'

It was the longest diatribe she'd ever uttered and it brought the pub to a stunned silence.

He was surprised that his finger-prodding lecture on the evils of capitalism hadn't done the trick and was about to give up on her when he was tapped on the shoulder by a tall, heavily-built man who smiled down on him. (Horatio may have been a big character, but he was barely five feet six.)

'Hello brother, remember me, I'm a Kangaroo?' said the man, offering him his large, spade-sized hand.

Now strange things happened at the Bomb and Dagger, often involving Horatio himself, but being on the receiving end of this one threw him off balance for an instant.

'You don't remember me, do you?' continued the man, still smiling affably. 'Let me give you a clue – lodge meeting?'

'Oh, bloody 'ell, why didn't you say so?' Horatio replied, taking the man's hand and finding himself being subjected to some rather strange manipulations of his fingers and wrist, until the stranger's hand disappeared up Horatio's sleeve, leaving him somewhat alarmed.

'Oh, sorry,' he said, 'I shouldn't have done that; I forgot you're only a Calf yet and haven't been initiated into the sacred handshakes of our craft. Habit, I suppose. Sorry.'

'Good God, mun, you scared me then; is that one of the sacred handshakes then?'

'Yes, it is, but for Heaven's sake don't tell the Great Bison I did it, or he'll have my golden horns removed. I only 'ad 'em two months ago. Anyway, how the Devil are you? Last time I saw you was in the bar of the lodge,' remarked the man, resuming a more normal attitude.

Horatio began to settle down and looked automatically at the almost empty pint glass in front of him. The man spotted the glance and made amends by offering him another pint. He suggested they sit down in a quiet corner.

Returning from the bar, where Mavis told the stranger to 'Watch out for that bloke, 'e's not right in the 'ead,' thus breaking another record for extended conversation. The man settled down next to Horatio on a bench seat against the wall and sipped his beer, silently.

That Horatio was an aspiring Buffalo has already been made clear. We've seen that he hoped not only to climb the organisational ladder but to perhaps (you never know) benefit from his contact with fellow Buffaloes. Such organisations bring about a natural sense of fellowship and it was this that he enjoyed, as well as the beer. You scratch my back and I'll scratch yours is, after all, very brotherly, even Communist, really.

Whilst the man had been getting the beer, Horatio wondered how to respond to him; for the life of him, he couldn't really remember who he was. If he was a Kangaroo he was a fairly senior Buffalo and Horatio didn't want to make a mess of this new 'contact'.

The difference between Communist brotherly love and that practiced by the Buffaloes is that the Buffaloes are generally middle class business people and better off than the Brethren. So asking a favour of a Buffalo could involve something more substantial than would result from asking one of the Brethren. A favour from one of the latter was more likely to be a fag or a pint of beer. A favour from a Buffalo could be much more worthwhile.

It should not be thought that only 'posh' people joined the Buffaloes. If this were so, Horatio wouldn't be there. And neither would a small handful of other men who earned their living by the sweat of their brows, although some of these were also well off, such as Abertwp's farmers. One such man was Eli, the Kangaroo. It was Eli who was sitting next to him.

He was indeed a farmer, albeit on a small scale, and was lucky enough to have a farm down in the floor of the valley where the grass was good and he could keep a dairy herd.

The two of them said little during their first pint. It was clear that each was sizing up the other. But drinking beer is easy, especially when financed by a well-off Kangaroo. So they got through a reasonable amount, Eli introducing himself more fully at last.

That beer loosens the tongue and softens the brain is well

known and thus it was that somehow or other Horatio got carried away describing the home he'd made for himself and the projects he'd undertaken – omitting completely any mention of his main occupation as the driver of a Volvo Mk IV ash cart.

Perhaps it was because he wanted to demonstrate a common interest, a point of connection, with Eli that he expressed his especial pride in the garden he cultivated. He itemised the crops he grew most years and, it has to be said, exaggerated rather stupidly the quantities he produced.

Somehow or other, Eli seemed to get the idea that Horatio was a small, struggling market gardener, judging by the sheer quantity and variety of vegetables he claimed to be growing. In fact, Eli was amazed at Horatio's claims:

'How that man manages to grow all that stuff in a tiny back garden in Slaughterhouse Terrace is beyond me,' he concluded in a sentiment verging on hero worship.

Horatio had done it again: persuaded someone that he was not only worthy of that person's admiration but deserving of their help. We remember that help came once before from a Buffalo in the shape of a length of copper pipe for his conservatory, so he began to wonder what help might come from Eli, if enough hints were dropped.

Although fellowship is encouraged in the Buffaloes, hierarchy is still respected. For example, a Calf, like Horatio, should think twice about nudging up against the Great Bison in the bar, slapping him on the back and cracking a dirty joke. A certain pecking order is maintained and respected at all times.

It was therefore not surprising that Horatio presented our friend Eli with a slight difficulty – an inversion of their hierarchy in fact. Should a senior member fraternise with a junior one?

Whatever the correct protocol, their drinking session had inspired in farmer Eli a desire to help Horatio with his horticulture, but he wasn't sure how to broach the idea.

Specifically, Eli had not long been promoted to the degree of Kangaroo, whereas Horatio was still on the first rung of the ladder, a Calf, which didn't even have a degree. In fact Horatio wasn't even a Wallaby, a junior Kangaroo.

Eventually Eli broached the subject:

'Look, we're both in the agriculture business and I know how 'ard it can be starting up, so I'd like to help you out. I've got something that'll really bring on your veg: manure. I bet you don't have enough to keep that garden of yours in proper shape. Fancy some?'

Horatio was delighted. 'You bet! Don't get much in the way of muck in our place,' he replied, with a chuckle. Gladys may not have wholeheartedly agreed with that statement, but her idea of muck was not her husband's idea of muck. What she called muck, he usually called dust or the natural results of honest labour – brick dust, sawdust, oil, paint splashes, earth from the garden, off-cuts of wood, etc.

'That's settled then, I'm glad I can help a fellow agriculturalist. I'll send the boy round with some in a few days' time.'

And so they parted: the Kangaroo pleased with himself at helping out another Buffalo and our Calf delighted to be getting some good stuff from the farm.

Horatio left the Bomb and Dagger saying to himself with an inner smile:

'Boy, that's bloody great! You watch the veg I'll get next year. Marvellous stuff muck. Can't 'ave enough of it.'

He returned to Slaughterhouse Terrace clearly pleased, which made Gladys worry. 'What was he up to now?' she wondered. She recognised that inner smile and it meant trouble usually. But days went by and nothing untoward happened. Horatio was constantly in a good mood and, strangely, kept working in the garden almost continually. He had almost dug over the whole plot, which was odd.

'This isn't right; he's up to something,' Gladys told herself.

The only clue to what might be happening was not so much the well-dug soil, but an area of cleared, flattened soil in the furthest corner of the veg patch, near the shed of Pisa, as if he was preparing to put something there. But what? Not another shed, surely?

'You're not going to build another bloody monstrosity, are you, I couldn't stand it,' she pleaded.

'Don't you worry, bach, nothing like that. Just you wait and see.'

This oft-repeated phrase 'just you wait and see' was one Gladys had heard many times and it filled her with dread. She now knew that he was indeed up to something. It was as though Horatio had said 'Trust me.' It never rang true somehow. Such words never pacified, they terrified.

Two days later, Horatio was bowling down the streets of Abertwp with his trusty crew in the Mk IV. He was lucky he was in work and not at home, because unknown to him, at around 11 o'clock, a very large tractor appeared outside number 47, pulling an enormous trailer piled high with manure.

It had stopped outside the wrong house of course, Horatio's being 74. The young lad driving it knocked on the door, which was answered by a small old man in slippers and a dressing gown.

'Mr Evans? I got a load for you. Where shall I dump it?'

'Nah, I'm not Evans, lad. He's the nutter across the road at 74. This is 47. What d'you mean, a load? A load of what?'

'Manure mate, manure. This bloke Evans ordered it for his business.'

'Well I bloody well didn't. It's definitely for that nutter in 74.'

'So where shall I dump it then? Can't see a back lane anywhere.'

'If it's manure, just dump it in the front of the 'ouse, that's what I do when I gets a load of coal.'

And the man at number 47 closed the door very slowly with the broadest grin he had brought into play for a long while, chuckling into his Bronchitis.

The lad climbed back into the tractor, reversed it and the trailer down the street and up onto the pavement where the load slipped down into the small front 'garden' – actually a patch of faded grass and two flower pots. The so-called front gardens in Slaughterhouse Terrace were tiny: no more than three feet in depth; just enough to delineate the private properties from the public pavement.

Farmers are a funny lot. Being used to driving enormous machines over rough ground, the odd bump here and there is not only ignored, it is not even registered. They get used to being in natural surroundings and find roads, pavements and even rows of houses unnatural and undeserving of as much care as a town-dweller might consider appropriate.

That the load hadn't completely left his trailer was of concern for the lad driving the tractor, because he didn't want to take any of it back. So he continued to move the tractor and trailer back and fore in order that every bit of muck he'd brought ended up somewhere, even if townsfolk wouldn't think it the best or appropriate place.

Once the front garden at number 74 was full, the only place it could go was the pavement, and then the road; although he did try hard to pile the stuff higher and higher in the garden to avoid too much spilling out onto the townsfolk's precious pavements.

Satisfied he had done what he was asked to do, the lad drove off at some speed, smoke billowing from the tractor's vertical exhaust and the trailer bouncing joyfully as though pleased to have been relieved of its distasteful contents.

Those contents were now four feet high in front of the

house (covering the lower half of the window) and the rest was spreading volcanically out into the road: a Mount Vesuvius of manure with steam rising like the clouds from the top of that very mountain. The pavement, of course, was totally impassable. If the smell of burning rope and creosote had upset the customers in Gwen's café, this was much worse.

It so happened that at this moment, the Horatio Express had stopped at the depot for Terry to pick up some spare fags from his locker. The Express was outside with its engine running, ready to speed off on the rest of its round. Terry seemed to be taking his time for some reason and emerged after several minutes, grinning broadly.

'We've got a change of orders, mates. We've gotta stop the round, pick up a flat-bed lorry and clear up a mess. Some idiot's gone an' dumped tons of crap in the middle of a road! It needs shiftin'. It's all 'ere on this bit o' paper from the boss. Bit of overtime for us tonight,' he sniggered, as he climbed into the cab.

Horatio, drilled into executing emergency orders from his army days, reversed the ash cart into its bay in the depot and jumped into an old flat-bed lorry that was not used much. It took a bit of coaxing to start, but start it eventually did. Terry chucked three shovels into the back of it.

'This 'eap o' junk is only fit for picking up crap from the street,' he commented. 'Where's the job slip, Flash?'

Terry hadn't looked at the sheet, but when Horatio did his foot slipped off the pedal and the old lorry stalled. He was left staring straight ahead, his breathing almost stopped.

'Bloody 'ell, this is my place! I know what this is. Oh, God! C'mon, this is serious, boys, it's outside our bloody 'ouse!'

The lorry reluctantly took off, shovels sliding and bouncing about in the back, and entered Slaughterhouse Terrace.

The scene was not a pretty one: the town's one policeman

(Police Constable Eustace by name, 'Useless' by nickname) was standing in the middle of the street hoping some traffic would drive down it so he could turn it back. There were few opportunities for Useless to impose his magisterial powers on the people (especially drivers) of Abertwp. He was enjoying himself in anticipation of exerting his authority.

Useless had been in the job for years, but he had never fully decided which side of the socio-political fence he was on: was he supposed to be looking after the interests, the peace and the quiet of his fellow voters, or was he supposed to be enforcing the wishes of the faceless ones in political power? He decided that in the end he was an enforcer, a term he liked using. This was the word that had seeped into his subconscious on this occasion.

Neighbours had gathered around the steaming heap, handkerchiefs over noses, discussing how bad things were getting these days with fly-tipping.

'D'you know, I saw an old mattress dumped up by the canal last week, which was disgusting, but I never thought someone would fly tip onto our bloody 'ouses!' moaned one depressed woman, whose opinion of her fellow citizens had now plummeted to an all-time low.

Of Gladys there was no sign: either she was incapacitated indoors, or she was out. Luckily for her, she was at her mam's, but her return by bus wouldn't be long. It would stop outside Gwen's café and an odorous hint of what had been dumped over her front garden may well waft towards her down the wind.

Horatio's lorry drove strangely slowly up to the offending heap and stopped several yards short of it, as though nervous of the thing. Jumping down from the cab, Horatio imposed his will immediately, by shouting at everyone to clear off so he and the lads could sort things out.

That he was particularly fired up by the incident could be measured pretty accurately by the angle at which his hat had been pushed backwards on his head, revealing most of his forehead. This part of his anatomy was rarely seen by the public, being normally reserved for his wife only, and only then in private. But it was unmistakeable that the white 'tide mark' caused by the lack of sun on the higher slopes of his forehead was now visible.

Both Iolo and Terry had long learned that when this white area could be seen, they shouldn't mess with Horatio: he meant business. They had occasionally discussed the issue. Iolo, the more mature of the two, reckoned such warning signs were often seen in nature – such as the fur of a cat rising up when angry. Terry added the example of baboons' bright red bottoms, which showed he hadn't really understood the thing

Horatio's shouting did not sit well with PC Useless, who was still enjoying the rare exercise of his powers. But when he realised with great pleasure that it was Horatio who would have to sort out this stinking mess and that it was Horatio's house that had been chosen for this apparent fly-tipping, he relented somewhat. Both men had clashed before: Useless and Horatio belonging on opposite sides of society, Useless imposing the status quo and Horatio trying to wreck it.

'I 'ave to remind you, Mr Hevans, that I am in charge 'ere and if anyone's gonna be told to clear off it'll be me that tells 'em. Anyway, I 'ave to collect as much hevidence as I can while it's still fresh, as it were!' he chuckled. 'Some idiot's responsible for this fly-tipping, not to mention causin' an obstruction. I hunderstand that this is your 'ouse? In which case you may be able to sue the perpetrator for compensation, when I do catch 'im that is and nowt's more certain than that.'

This confrontation with Useless was interrupted by the old man from number 47 crossing the street, still in his dressing gown and slippers, waving his walking stick.

'Don't wave that at me,' warned Useless, 'it's an offensive weapon, and I'm a hofficer of the law.'

'Don't be daft, mun, I'm just going to tell you who did it, but if you don wanna know I'll bugger off.'

'Now then, now then, don' be funny with me. If you 'ave hevidence I need to know. Who was it?'

'It was that lad from Eli's farm; 'e done it, I saw 'im.'

This statement stunned Horatio. The good deed from the Kangaroo was about to go pear-shaped and very public – and it already had a bad smell to it. How could he complain about this mess to a fellow Buffalo, and a more senior one at that?

It was touch and go whether he could maintain his image of reassuring leadership as this sank in. At the same time, he noticed just how far up the window the heap was piled. For once, his brain froze and there was a serious danger that his body might too. He now realised how awful the situation was but he also realised that it wasn't entirely his fault: it was the Kangaroo that had done this, albeit indirectly.

His allegiances mixed, he decided that attack was the best form of defence.

'Look, me and the lads 'ave been told to sort this out, so why don' you all let us get on with it. It's only a pile o' crap, after all. We'll soon shift it.'

With which he jumped into the lorry and began backing it towards the heap, revving loudly so as to show clearly that it was time for the onlookers to clear off whilst he got stuck in. His two colleagues had already armed themselves with shovels and were ready for work. He was right: action was needed, not words.

It hasn't been mentioned previously, but besides considering refuse-collecting to be an altruistic social calling (ideal for a communist) he also considered it to be an emergency service. In fact, he had only recently asked his foreman if the telephone number of his house could be advertised in all phone boxes, telephone directories and shop windows of the town and officially classed as the fourth emergency service.

'But you 'aven't even got a bloody phone!' yelled the foreman with a wide grin on his face, 'is that what you're after, a phone?' he queried, laughing. 'That's a bloody good one, that is. 'Horatio bloody Evans, the fourth emergency service of Abertwp!' Hah-hah-hah, hah-hah, Oh that's bloody good that is!'

'The bloody council can install one, can't they? I bet you've got one! And I bet you make private calls on it,' Horatio asserted, somewhat downcast by the foreman laughing at him.

The depot foreman dismissed Horatio's attempt to get a free phone and raise his social standing. But clearing up the mountain of manure certainly gave Horatio's argument some weight, he thought to himself.

'After all, what would these silly sods do if we weren't 'ere to rescue 'em?' he told himself. 'We're a bloody rescue service, we are.'

'Sorry, but I can't allow you to move this stuff,' declared Useless, 'this is hevidence.'

'Listen, do you lot want this muck shifted or not?' challenged Horatio.

All murmured affirmatively. Useless had been overruled.

'Alright then, shift it, but I need all your names as witnesses,' he declared, opening his little black book, which until that time had rarely seen daylight.

The lads set to. It was slow, smelly work and the stuff was as sticky and as slimy as – well, manure.

'What we needs is a machine,' suggested Iolo.

Horatio had an idea: 'Carry on lads, while I go to the Bomb and use Geraint's phone; I know who'll give us an 'and with this.'

And off Horatio went, with a fast, determined step to phone the Kangaroo and ask for help. His pleas were answered by

Eli himself who appeared only minutes later at the end of the street, driving a tractor with a scoop on the front.

Nothing was said between Eli and Horatio. They hardly acknowledged each other. The latter realised he'd exaggerated his horticultural needs and the former had been overly generous to Horatio and overly trusting of his own farmhand.

The pile on the road and then that on the pavement was soon in the lorry. But the still significant proportion in Horatio's front garden remained.

'Can't do much about that,' opined Eli. 'Yer gonna 'ave to shift it yerself, mate.'

At this point he still hadn't got down from the tractor, clearly embarrassed at the misunderstanding that had resulted in this mess. So he turned his vehicle round and zoomed off, muttering to himself that this Buffalo Calf would never make a Wallaby.

Were Horatio's future prospects as a rising Buffalo now in the balance? He certainly felt so. But the Kangaroo felt unable to mention any of this to the Great Bison because he too was not innocent. That stupid farmhand of his would be taken down a peg or two when he got back to the farm.

The Council lorry took off and dumped the offending material back at Eli's farm, although nothing to this effect was officially recorded in the depot's records, for fear of tracing the source of the stuff and thereby satisfying Constable Useless' inquisitiveness.

There remained just half a ton of manure for Horatio to dispose of. It had always been destined for his back garden and that was where it was going to go.

'Listen lads, we've always 'ad a bloody good laugh together and you're my best mates; give me an 'and to shift this round the back, eh?'

This, thought Terry and Iolo, was asking a bit much. But ash cart crews stick together so a deal was struck: Terry would get 40 fags and Iolo some new harmonica music.

Iolo didn't live very far, so he brought his own wheelbarrow. Horatio had one too, of a sort. But they needed a third.

Jones' Emporium (Suppliers of All Things Sanitary to the Gentry) had a pile of them in front of the shop and Horatio managed somehow to arrange the loan of one with the promise he would promote Jones' Emporium as an official supplier 'by appointment' to the Abertwp Town Council.

Gladys, meanwhile, returned. She had passed a pleasant day with her mam, and was in a good mood. For once her chest wasn't too tight and her outlook was almost normal. This changed immediately when she saw the mess in her front garden and smelled the smell in her living room. There was no other way to get the stuff from the front of the house to the back garden without wheeling it through the house. Being of a semi-liquid nature, and the route requiring a number of sharp turns, notably around the settee, the stuff had slopped over the edges of the wheelbarrows and was building up on various parts of the floor and furniture.

To be fair, Horatio had taken up the mats, a worthy act, but had done little else to mitigate against manure-covered linoleum. The settee seemed to take the worst of it, but the sideboard was also a victim, not of manure, but of wheelbarrow gouges, all at exactly the same height.

Gladys turned round without saying a word, nipped into next door to take a few deep whiffs of Neville's Oxygen bottle, and hurried with both girls to the bus stop again. They sought refuge and renewed solace at her mam's.

This left the lads plenty of leeway to carry on with the task, ignoring the finer points of furniture damage, manure build-up and the smell.

Thus it was that Horatio's horticultural and Buffalo ambitions took a bit of a bashing. But he wasn't finished yet. Once dumped in the garden, the pile of manure was so enormous that it occupied a good proportion of the entire plot. It had been piled high in the front of the house and therefore didn't look too bad, but once gravity pulled at the unrestrained volume in the back, it spread out, like a landslide.

The relatively modest patch of ground he had cleared in one corner was completely drowned in the stuff. As for the state of his garden overall, it had been devastated by the to-ing and fro-ing of the wheelbarrows. Whilst the carrots, broccoli and potatoes had disappeared under the ever-expanding manure heap, the rest bore the deep furrows of three heavy wheelbarrows and three sets of Council-issue boots.

At the end of the exercise, Horatio stood proudly in the middle of what was left of his horticultural 'business' with hands on his hips, surveying the heap with pride.

'If that doesn't grow stuff, nothing will,' he thought to himself.

Iolo couldn't help but ask what Horatio was going to do with such a mountainous pile of dung.

'No problem, lad, I'll dig it in. That's the place for muck, in the soil.'

That he was already looking to the future was impressive: a sure sign that his determination and vision were undimmed.

There was still no sign of Gladys and the girls and he was secretly glad they weren't there. Although the heap had been moved from the front of the house, liberating their little bit of front garden, he, like many men, hadn't thought of the aesthetics of the result.

What had been a small, dried-up patch of grass with a few flowerpots was now a sticky, greenish mess. It had been impossible to scoop up all the stuff and much remained, stuck, as it were in the grass.

As for the flowerpots, they had disappeared into shards that had been scooped up with the manure and were buried somewhere in the volcanic heap out the back.

On the walls and window of the front of the house, the high tide mark of the steaming heap was still clear to see.

These were details to Horatio. Unfortunately, they were not details to Gladys, but she was yet to see them. Iolo, the most sensitive of the three did try and point out that they ought to wash down the front of the house, but Horatio, as was his habit, was concentrating on the bigger, strategic issues.

Leaders tend to do this.

The Horticultural Adventure

Now THAT OUR hero had such a large pile of manure, the issue occupying his mind was how to incorporate it into the soil of his small garden. For several years he'd nurtured the idea of a using mechanical cultivator on his plot: in fact he had one – albeit missing a minor part, the engine.

He had been given what was the 'business end' of the cultivator by one of Gladys' brothers, Bryn, who was a mechanic with his own small workshop business; but he'd kept the engine and thrown out the rest. The blades were intact, if bent, and the control cables were missing. It was rusty, so that nothing actually moved. But Bryn reckoned that if his 'nutty' brother-in-law wanted the thing, he could have it.

'No-one else would be daft enough to try and use it. Without an engine, it's useless,' Bryn reasoned.

'Nothing that can't be fixed,' insisted Horatio. 'I'm not a bloody capitalist sod like you who can afford to buy a new one of these. The proletariat 'ave to make do with what they can get,' he declared to as he had taken away the rusty contraption's parts.

Bryn hardly spoke when Horatio was around, in order to save embarrassing his sister. It took him a huge effort of will to stay silent. Ever since he'd first met Horatio at Gladys' wedding, he thought his new brother-in-law was a dangerous idiot. He was protective of his younger sister and was often tempted to go down to Abertwp and 'sort out that idiot.' We can perhaps understand Bryn's attitude when hearing Horatio call him 'a capitalist sod' at the very moment he was giving Horatio the remains of the mechanical cultivator.

To our hero this was not meant to give offence. He was merely educating Bryn in the problems of the proletariat. That Bryn might be offended, would in any case be seen by any well-indoctrinated Communist as indicative of someone with excessive selfish capitalist interests. People had to be told the truth, Horatio told himself, even if it hurt. Bryn had to be converted from his misguided ways.

The rusty bits of the cultivator had been stored in Horatio's leaning shed of Pisa for years. Now was the time to bring it out into the full light of day – its moment had come.

It needed an engine and he knew where to get one – round the back of the Cwmtwrch Garage ('23½ hour breakdown service – everyone needs a break – in God we trust, the rest pay cash').

The garage was a peculiar place, built on a steep hillside overlooking Abertwp. It had wonderful views of the town, the proprietor, Will Thomas, spending a lot of time appreciating it. He was not, and he was the first to admit it, a born worker. He was more of a poet-philosopher than a mechanic, reckoning that it was better to take time out and look at the God-given view than work himself to death. There was a poet in him somewhere, in fact the appreciation of poetry ran in the family.

He was also of a generous nature. His particular brand of philosophy was very benign and based on everyone sharing what he had with others. The Communist Brethren had tried several times to tempt him into the Party but he was an individualist, preferring to develop his own brand of communism, although he never called it that.

Basically, he was lazy, his wife maintained, and far too generous because he really hated the process of asking customers for payment. You would think that 'forgetting' to ask customers for payment would ensure that the garage was very popular but since it took him ages to do anything, most customers preferred paying someone else in order to enjoy the confidence that their job would actually get done. Will explained away his pecuniary reluctance by claiming that his branch of the Celts belonged to the ancient Beaker Folk, not given to hard work, preferring pure artistic creativity to hard graft.

'Artists and philosophers have a tough time of it with their wives and customers,' he thought, 'they just don't understand us.'

Will's philosophy of benevolence was a blessing for Horatio, who turned up at the hillside garage humming a Welsh hymn, deliberately chosen to endear him to Will. He didn't bother looking for Will in the garage workshop, or down in the service pit; he knew Will would be looking out over the valley, philosophising and thanking Heaven, he was Welsh.

'Shwmae, Will?' he enquired.

This familiar form of Welsh greeting was pleasing to Will who was a native Welsh speaker and he replied at length to Horatio's enquiry in his native tongue, confusing his listener no end. He guessed Will was romancing about the view, because he didn't take his eyes off the horizon, waving his arms about to express his love of the scene and reciting Welsh poetry.

Will's father had been a frequent competitor at the Abertwp Eisteddfod and was once a runner-up in the poetry prize. Will knew his father's poem by heart. His wife did too – she'd heard it every day for years.

'Will, sorry to interrupt you, bach, but 'ave you still got that old motorbike engine out the back – you know the one, it came off that bike that crashed last year up on the Twmp?'

'Oh, that damned thing, aye, it's still there, rusting out the back. Why? Do you fancy doing it up?'

'Aye, I'd like to 'ave a bash at it. I got a really good use for it and Gladys would be glad if I could 'ave it.'

Using Gladys' name was applying extra emotional leverage to Horatio's request, a softening-up tactic often used by negotiators, he thought. Gladys was very friendly with Will's wife and they both went to the same chapel – Bethesda. Gladys confided in her as the only woman who understood what it was to be married to an idiot. Will, Gladys concurred, fell into this category quite nicely. He never seemed to be doing much and as a result their means were meagre: all because he was a romantic and loved poetry.

'Go on then, pick it up if you want. I don' want it. But it don' work, you know.'

The Mk IV ash cart drove to the Cwmtwrch Garage next day and transported the precious engine to Slaughterhouse Terrace.

Horatio's confidence was again at a high point. Although he knew a bit about engines (from his army days) it was a long time since he'd stripped one down and done anything serious with it – such as adapting it to power a cultivator for which it was never intended. This was a powerful motorbike engine and totally unsuited to gently turning over the soil. But if he could get this thing going, there were no limits to his horticultural ambitions. Kangaroo Eli would be impressed and the potential rift between them over the manure affair may be healed.

There was no room to work on the engine in the shed of Pisa, so he had to use whatever flat surface he could find. This was the dining table. Already missing its centre leaf, scored and scarred from the fireplace project, it was looking pretty sad now. The family didn't use it much, except at Christmas and for Horatio doing his pools, so there would be little or no interruption to the family routine (he decided).

Gladys and the girls were still technically away but were actually on the number 34 bus returning to Abertwp from Swansea. As they got down, Gladys looked around nervously, wondering if the street had been cleared of the manure and if any crowds were still outside her house. She also sniffed to check if anything else had been polluting the air. Relieved that all seemed quiet, but still tense, she and the girls walked slowly and deliberately down the centre of the street like three cowboys about to clean up the town.

They entered number 74 just as the engine was draining into Gladys' washing up bowl, which was filling with foul-smelling, black oil.

'Oh, dear God, what are you doing now?' she pleaded? 'That's my one and only bowl and my one and only dining table! And it still stinks in 'ere!'

This was strong stuff from Gladys; she was normally so passive, saying hardly anything. Horatio had got used to her silence, but the manure episode must have got to her. She had somehow found the strength to push back at Horatio, something for which he was totally unprepared, especially when endorsed by one of the girls.

'Now look, woman, I got lots o' good muck out the back, and if you'll just be patient, I'm gonna fit this engine to the bloody cultivator, turn over the soil as farmers do, and next year we'll have the best bloody veg and plenty of it. Trust me.'

If only he hadn't used those last two words! He may have got away with it. Gladys and the girls trusted Horatio less than they trusted their local councillors – and he was one. But 'trust me' was a sure sign of impending disaster.

'Tell you what, why don' you all go and stay with your sister Doris in Swansea? Nice bit o' sand down by there on the beach.'

'We know there's nice sand there; some of it is sticking your bloody conservatory together,' cried Gladys as she sank onto the settee, from which she stood up fairly quickly because where she had laid her head on the arm, was a splattering of manure that stank strongly. 'I've only just come back from Mam's, now you're chucking us out again!'

For some reason, probably known only to organic chemists, the smell of manure seems to linger, even when washed out with bleach, which is what Terry had done to the settee. It certainly brightened up the back of the item, which was now almost cream (in patches), quite a different colour from the rest, which was dark brown. Perhaps the muck had soaked into cracks in the linoleum: Horatio wasn't sure, but Gladys and the girls reckoned the place smelled worse than a cow shed.

As any farmer will tell you, if you're working with muck all day, you don't notice the smell – eventually. This is probably the stage that Horatio and his two colleagues had reached – they had developed immunity to it.

It was not, however, an immunity shared by Gladys and the girls. They didn't spend more than five minutes in the room before all three went upstairs, packed two suitcases and caught the next bus to Swansea – again. Horatio, ever the generous head of the household, gave them the bus fare. He reckoned Gladys spent more time on the 34 bus than in the house.

'At least it'll give me some time to sort out this little baby,' he said, grinning and rubbing his oily hands. 'She'll feel better when this is done and the garden's tidy again. Women just don't understand these things.'

We shan't go into the details involved in the dismantling of the engine, the battle he had with rust (solved by immersing it in their tin bath full of petrol, which raised safety questions all its own) or the fact that once reassembled, it presented Horatio with significant problems as to how to attach it to the remnant of the mechanical cultivator he had in his shed.

Suffice to say, that with extremely reluctant help from his

brother-in-law, Bryn, he managed to have it welded to the rusty remains of the cultivator and all was ready for commissioning. How Bryn kept his temper during this work was, even to him, a total mystery. Having Horatio breathing down his neck during the operation was almost intolerable, especially when his welding work was criticised. Bryn felt like welding Horatio to the thing!

The commissioning of the horticultural wonder-machine took place, unfortunately, on a Sunday. Bearing in mind that Sunday in Wales was a hallowed and essentially silent day, the roar of an engine was frowned upon by the voters of Abertwp. To a secular Communist like Horatio, however, this seemed nonsense and rather than deterring him from making a noise, he saw it as his duty to make some.

Gladys, eventually returned from a three-day stay in Swansea, was distressed at Horatio's attitude and expressed her shame to her sister-in-law as they made their way to the Bethesda Chapel that morning. It was an event to which she looked forward each week, not only to make her peace with her Maker, but for the fellowship it provided. In fact, it was pretty well the only occasion when she could feel at ease, because she was doing something just for herself and which she enjoyed. It was also an occasion when she felt safe; the old chapel provided a haven, both physically and emotionally. It was neutral territory, never to be spoiled by Horatio and his secular theories. In logistical terms it was also easy to get to: Bethesda Chapel was in the next street to her own.

Sitting in her allotted pew alongside her sister-in-law that morning, both of them resplendent in feathered hats, Gladys couldn't help feeling, in spite of her liberal use of perfume, that she was not smelling her freshest, somehow. The smell of manure seemed to have clung to her clothes; or perhaps her nose just couldn't rid itself of the lingering molecules of the stuff.

But they enjoyed singing the first hymn, 'Hapus Wyf I' (Happy am I), to a favourite tune of Gladys' although she hated the words with a vengeance. The hymn over, they sat down and, with the organ winding down to a solemn drone, as though exhaling its last breath, the visiting preacher, the Rev. Goronwy Roberts stood up in the pulpit and stared out threateningly at the congregation.

Gladys suddenly had a fleeting and un-Christian realisation that the preacher was from Llanelli, the town from whence came all her grief and sadness; the very town that was responsible for the birth of Horatio ap Llewelyn Evans. She tried to put the thought to one side and 'think Christian'. But it was difficult.

'He even haunts me in chapel,' she said to herself.

But in spite of making a determined Christian effort not to think about it, Llanelli was not to be ignored. Somewhere not far away, someone had started up an engine that was making the most infernal noise. Defying many attempts to start it, the engine on the horticultural wonder-machine had at last spluttered deafeningly into life and was coughing out fumes like a North Atlantic destroyer laying a smokescreen.

'Oh, God, help us!' she inwardly groaned, 'I know what that noise is and I know exactly where it's coming from. He's started that engine of his.'

The preacher didn't employ a loud voice, at least initially. He was one of the fiery Welsh preachers who always began quietly and slowly, beguiling and coaxing his congregations with a seductive mix of empathy and admissions that he too was a sinner.

He would follow this gentle, forgiving seduction by a sudden crescendo of condemnation for their sins (but not his), before finally damning his entire congregation to eternal Hellfire if they weren't more Christian during the coming week. If his blood pressure held out, he would even thump the pulpit and punch the air to add emphasis to his curse upon the wicked before him.

Whatever one's spiritual inclinations, such orators never failed to provide a good emotional ride. The pleasant feelings congregations felt when exiting a chapel may have been as much due to the emotional relief that came from experiencing such a roller-coaster as in surviving the damnations of Hell itself.

But this time the preacher's strategy was not working. The noise of the spluttering 250cc engine as it powered the cultivator was winning the competition for the congregation's ears. It was also winning the congregation's noses, because the chapel was downwind of the garden at 74 Slaughterhouse Terrace and was being treated to a good dose of unburned petrol fumes and exhaust gases.

As the preacher steadily increased his volume to match the cultivator, looking less confident by the minute, the congregation became restive. Gladys was the most unsettled of all, receiving puritanical looks from several quarters, not least of all from her adjacent sister-in-law. Gladys decided to leave. As she did so, she could swear the preacher's words were meant just for her:

'Damned are those who do not keep the Sabbath to keep it holy. Damned saith the Lord. Damned I say!'

'Alright, alright, I got the message,' she thought to herself, feeling the glare of condemnation from both preacher and congregation as she stumbled, blushing deeply, out the door.

Entering the street, she ran the gauntlet of numerous neighbours who were standing on their doorsteps discussing the awful disturbance and the clouds of smoke coming from number 74.

They were mostly women, whose body language said much. They had all folded their arms under their breasts and their chins seemed to have been pulled in somewhat, the effect being a communal attempt at silent condemnation, with breasts that were tucked in, ready for action. They adopted this tense, judgemental stance in pairs of adjacent doorways. They had laid on a guard of shame past which Gladys had to scurry.

The men, though fewer, had gathered in a group in the centre of the street outside the house and were mostly laughing. The old man from 47 was with them, still in his dressing gown, waving his stick and shouting comments about 'that nutter in 74'.

This was not the sort of quiet Sunday morning Gladys wanted or deserved. Her nerves were in a terrible state and she really needed rest. Not knowing whether to smile shyly at her female judges or to try and complete her walk without looking to left or right, she at last made it to the front door, which was wide open, exhaust fumes drifting out into the street.

In the garden, the Battle of the Somme had been faithfully reproduced. The machine, being equipped now with an engine five times as powerful as the one with which it was born, was churning up everything into which it came into contact. Any vegetables that had survived the wheelbarrows and council boots were in shreds; deep trenches had been created across the garden in a strangely random way. The reason was simple: it was out of control.

The machine was doing its stuff, but it was too powerful to handle. Horatio was committed to hanging on as best he could as it ploughed its way across the plot, only changing direction when it hit something, at which point it dug itself in, deeper and deeper until it hit a large stone or other substantial subterranean obstacle. The topology thus created was amazing. Hills and valleys, some quite deep had been created everywhere.

One particular trench, the most impressive and most reminiscent of a battlefield, was about three feet deep and extended several yards towards the leaning shed of Pisa, but had luckily missed it. Instead, it had continued onwards until it hit the foundations of the neighbour's wall. At which point it dived ever deeper, which was precisely the clever mechanism that Barnes Wallis employed for destroying the dams in Germany. His bomb also dived deeper once it struck the dam wall, ensuring the destruction of its foundations.

The manure heap, meanwhile, remained in solemn control of its corner of the garden. None of it had moved or been moved. But now the mound was just another mound amongst many and it didn't stand out as much.

If you didn't know him, the look on Horatio's face seemed to indicate that he was enjoying himself. But to a seasoned observer, his face showed he was terrified. He had an otherworldly, fixed grin on his face, as though lockjaw had set in. His eyes had within them a look of pitiful appeal, begging for help.

The poor man was now the victim of the terrifying machine, condemned never to let go, yet unable to stop. The string he had used to replace the missing steel control cables had let him down. The 'thing' was now a monster, destined to patrol the garden forever, creating havoc and destruction wherever it went. Horatio had become the Flying Welshman of the horticultural world.

As the cultivator continued without mercy to drag him along behind it, it began its return journey from the other end of the garden at a depth of about two feet when it suddenly struck a stone and veered towards the leaning shed of Pisa.

The machine, not meeting any substantial obstacles, subterranean or otherwise, literally burrowed its way beneath the shed which seemed to explode in a cloud of matchsticks and dust. It was in ruins, having spilled out its entire contents (mainly tomato boxes) across the garden. His liberated British Railways shovel was the only item recognisable, lying in the one corner of the edifice that remained.

With a loud bang and much smoke, the fiendish contraption finally stopped when it was three feet down. The monster had overdone it. The crankshaft was broken and, having had its final fling, had given up, expired, shot its bolt. Then something odd happened. The pit it had dug began filling with water which appeared to be fizzing like pop in a bottle. In his state of shock he thought it looked quite attractive. What happened next was not attractive: it had first struck a water pipe and then the gas main.

It was at this moment that Gladys appeared, smoking her habitual Woodbine. Suffice to say the explosion was fairly loud and she was thrown backwards onto the manure heap unhurt but shocked. Her fag was nowhere to be seen.

The ignited gas produced a rather beautiful flame that was quite impressive. Luckily, the machine had not severed the pipe completely and the water and soil were partially blocking the break. The fire brigade did a splendid job and gas supplies were restored by late evening.

Horatio was disappointed. But at least the terror of the experience was over. After all that work on the engine all he had to show was a wrecked garden, no vegetables, no shed, and a gas flame thirty feet high. Not to mention that his reputation with his neighbours had now hit a new low. Mr Davies next door, the cage-fighter, had to be restrained by his wife and two men from 'fixing that bloke once and for all.'

'If there's one thing I've learned, boys,' he admitted in the Bomb and Dagger the next day, 'don't be taken in by a Kangaroo.'

His listeners now realised how far gone he really was.

No Surrender

W E BEGAN HORATIO'S story in Llanelli, where he was born. His parents Arthur and Lavender Evans maintained their peculiar relationship faithfully: Arthur stuck at it because he believed he had no alternative; Lavender because in spite of all the years that had passed, her sense of revenge had still not been satisfied.

Her parents, throughout this period, had steadfastly refused to contact her. The stories they were compelled to tell their friends and the rest of the family in order to perpetuate the lie that she was living in New Zealand, became ever more complex as a result.

They didn't go as far as forging false letters from Lavender (although they once bought some used New Zealand stamps) but the yarns about her allegedly successful life in the Antipodes with a brain surgeon had to be kept fresh and interesting. To do this, both of them had to constantly consult and rehearse their stories in order to ensure they didn't lay a trap for each other with conflicting 'facts'.

This constant strain on them may have led to Lavender's father deciding he'd had enough of the florist business and was going to sell up. It had been a good business and the generous price he got for it surprised him. They decided it would be best if they retired and moved away from the rest of the family in Bristol, thus relieving them of the need for constant story-telling.

They moved into a pleasant, but rather small bungalow, in

Weston-Super-Mare. They had decided to downsize, having had enough of keeping both a shop and a four-bedroomed house in Clifton. The bungalow was a clone of many similar ones in the street behind the sea front: painted white, it had a small front garden, a garage and a reasonably-sized back garden which would keep them quietly busy. The net financial result of this change was that they had quite a bit of spare cash.

Several months passed and they both agreed that retirement was good. It was as they were walking along the promenade one day that Lavender's mother looked across the Severn Estuary to south Wales and remarked:

'It's strange to think that somewhere over there is our daughter and our grandson. I am beginning to feel bad about not being in touch. Do you think we ought do something about it?'

This came out of the blue; she even surprised herself by suggesting it. Perhaps now that they were both comfortable, and living away from friends and relatives, they had subconsciously reassessed their relationship with their daughter. As they hadn't ever seen their grandson Horatio, except in some early photographs, their instinct for nurturing their offspring may have suddenly awakened.

So it was that Lavender received a surprise letter from her mother – perhaps 'surprise' is too mild a word: she had almost forgotten she had parents at all – suggesting that they visited Llanelli and their grandson.

Besides the unexpected element of receiving such a missive, the implications immediately washed over Lavender like a tidal wave. To show them the meagre house where she lived and the extremely strange house where their grandson lived was something she couldn't imagine happening without significant planning – if it were to happen at all. What on earth would her parents think?

It gave rise to a unique occasion: she asked Arthur to sit down with her and discuss something, a request he found distinctly unnerving. Brain-to-brain contact between them had long been sporadic, to say the least; when it had occasionally happened it usually resulted in one thought shooting past another as though mid-air contact should be avoided at all cost.

Suffice to say that once the idea had been spoken out loud, and a few days had passed, Lavender realised she had unknowingly missed her parents. And so she spoke tentatively in favour of seeing them again.

That her parents should then go on to meet Horatio was, however, another matter. Arthur and Lavender had visited him after the lean-over had been completed, and both had beaten a hasty retreat to Llanelli.

They hadn't seen anything like it before or since. Arthur was convinced his son was nuts, whereas Lavender was convinced they had let him down; that if Horatio's wife, Gladys and her family, had been more supportive his true talents would have come to the fore and his life in Abertwp would have been so different.

Eventually, letters were exchanged between Lavender and her parents and a date set for them to visit. Not having a spare room in Tinplate Terrace (Lavender alleged) her parents readily agreed it would be no inconvenience for them to stay at a hotel.

The visit sent Lavender into a spin. The house had to be cleaned from top to bottom and several DIY jobs that Arthur had been avoiding for years had to be completed - fast. In spite of hitting the targets she'd set for improving the house, she realised that there were two things that she could never improve – her neighbours and the neighbourhood.

One plan she hatched was to meet her parents on neutral territory, but Arthur wouldn't hear of it.

'There's nothing wrong with this place,' he insisted, 'if they're too stuck up to see where we lives they needn't come.'

Lavender's years of revenge had made its mark; kindly co-operation between the two of them was going to be difficult, especially for Arthur. He was sensing his own revenge.

But he hit on a plan of his own which pleased Lavender no end: he would spend a couple of days 'on holiday' in the shunting yard sheds where years ago he had found a warm place to lay his head and some friendly male companionship. That way, Lavender could weave whatever stories she liked about him and he would be away from the tension and artificiality that the visit was bound to generate.

As for her parents, seeing their genius grandchild, for that is how Lavender described Horatio, was another matter. They had written to him and received a short reply on a scrap of council notepaper to the effect that if his grandparents wanted to visit 74 Slaughterhouse Terrace, they were welcome provided they took him and his family as they found them.

'They can come 'ere if they want to, though it's taken 'em long enough,' he declared to Gladys, who, like Lavender, was dreading the experience.

Having previously booked into a hotel, Lavender's parents turned up in their large, green Rover car one Tuesday at midday. The car itself was enough to signal to the neighbours that something of note was happening. Rather than enhance Lavender's status, however, it diminished it.

'Told you she was stuck up,' the neighbours agreed.

Entering the house, her parents' behaviour was stiff and circumspect. Two pairs of English middle-class eyes scanned every corner, registering the quality of the ornaments, the carpets, pictures (of which there was only one, a reproduction of a view of the tinplate works at night) and finally the incomplete set of crockery and miscellaneous cutlery set out on the chintz-covered table (a strategically placed plate covering a deep stain).

We can imagine how difficult the conversation became once polite 'hellos' had been exchanged. It had been decades since they had seen each other or spoken.

Lavender's mother was the first to break the ice and pleasantly surprised her daughter by apologising for the way they had abandoned her after the birth of Horatio. Lavender was shocked and secretly pleased; up until that moment, she had been a lonely exile living in a foreign land; now she had found two other 'normal' English people who could perhaps understand her feelings and even support her.

Lavender made excuses for Arthur by saying he had had to work overtime. As though to smooth over his absence, she stressed what a good man he was and how appreciative she was of his substantial earning capacity. (She later wondered how she had managed to say these things about the husband she called a Welsh twerp.)

Tea was served and drunk. A Victoria sponge was consumed, notably by her father, and eventually the atmosphere relaxed.

Then, out of the blue, they announced to Lavender the news they had agreed on: they had lots of spare cash from the sale of the business and would like Lavender to have some. They also wanted to give some to their grandson, Horatio.

This softened the atmosphere immediately. Here, Lavender realised, could be her chance to rise out of the scruffy backwardness of Tinplate Terrace and seek a house in the tree-lined uplands of Llanelli's more desirable districts amongst people who knew what natural spaghetti was. Lavender, in spite of all the years of anger, revenge and sadness, suddenly lit up with optimism. But what was the catch? They said they also wanted Horatio to have some money.

Lavender and Arthur had had little to do with him since his marriage, Arthur saying that his son ought to be left alone to 'plough his own furrow'. Privately, Arthur thought his son needed psychiatric care and would rather keep his distance. As for Horatio's confusingly contradictory political activities, Arthur was genuinely worried; to him, anyone dabbling in such things was bound to be either nuts or devious or both.

Eventually, Lavender's parents left for their hotel at around 4 p.m. Their departure was witnessed by numerous housewives who suddenly and simultaneously found some work to do on their doorsteps. As the Rover pulled away from the kerb and she waved her parents goodbye, Lavender was able to smile at them for the first time for a long time.

'Now we'll see who has the last laugh,' she told herself with warm satisfaction.

Her parents' plan was to visit Horatio the following morning at Abertwp. They were not looking forward to it. The idea of visiting a dirty mining town did not attract them after living in the clean, whitewashed coastal resort of ozone-washed Weston-Super-Mare. In fact, when they got to their room at the hotel and closed their bedroom door, they were initially both silent about their impression of Tinplate Terrace.

'Not much of a place, is it?' her father eventually said, cautiously.

'I know; I think it's just awful. All those dirty, tiny houses and probably dirty tiny people in them too,' whispered her mother, in case anyone bugging the room heard her. This was epiphany time.

Neither parent wanted to really say what they felt about Lavender's standard of living except that something must be done to rescue her.

'She is our daughter, after all is said and done. There's been lots of water under the bridge; she's made her bed and has been lying in it. She mustn't count her chickens before they hatch, but blood is thicker than water.'

The liberally scattered aphorisms were a euphemistic way of saying what neither of them wanted to admit: they'd left their daughter in a mess all these years and they owed her something.

As for Horatio and his potential windfall, that was to be another thing altogether. Proud, independent and somewhat Bolshie, the thought of him accepting a gift from bourgeois grandparents who'd never bothered with him before was likely to be problematical, both philosophically and politically (notably the latter). Having money and, by definition, becoming a capitalist, would ruin his standing with the Brethren, a reputation that he had built up over many years – although it would improve his position with the Buffaloes. (This is the benefit of riding two horses at the same time, he observed.)

But the manure episode with the Kangaroo was beginning to set his mind against the Buffaloes. His ascent to the degree of Wallaby had not yet happened, although it was promised to be soon, and he was feeling a little let down.

As a result, he decided to specialise, for the time being at least, mostly in Communism and its close cousin Trade Unionism and nurture the Brethren's support. As an addendum to this confused non-decision, he told himself that if, on the other hand, any useful opportunities came from being a Wallaby he would still remain a Buffalo. To Horatio this (unaccountably) seemed to clear the air. He was to be a communist first with Buffalo leanings, which, really, is what he already was.

One characteristic of outstanding leaders is their ability to cope with uncertainty. In this case, however, Horatio's views were not only uncertain but polar opposites. Nevertheless he saw nothing wrong in being both a Buffalo and a Communist, or, as he had now decided, a Communist and a Buffalo. Genius is difficult to understand sometimes.

'We'll get that bloody red flag flying over Abertwp yet,' he decided, 'and if anything comes of the Buffs, I'm their man.'

To cut a long and painful story short, his grandparents' visit to 74 Slaughterhouse Terrace was not a success. One look at the place ensured that they were not only shocked but unable to comprehend what Horatio had been up to.

Before they entered the house, they noticed the high tide mark of the manure heap on the front window and walls and could smell the ground was still saturated with the stuff. A tour of the cottage revealed the strange, leaning wardrobe with the door missing in the girls' room; the smoking, cracked fireplace surrounded by torn wallpaper, missing skirting boards and two large, naked, plaster statues holding sculpted samples of Polyfilla.

As for the conservatory or lean-over, Horatio's grandfather jumped back into the living room as soon as he entered the edifice, fearing for his life in case the thing collapsed. (The girls' three lengths of wood were still supporting 'Jesus Walking on the Waters'.)

He did, however, cautiously poke his head around the door a second time to fully appreciate the bath arrangement with its long copper pipe, ending in a fine collection of brass 'adaptions'.

But it was the sight of the 'garden' that made him go pale. As his eyesight penetrated the distorting panes of mixed glass in miscellaneous scrap windows, he saw the battle of the Somme in miniature. In a corner, the manure heap sat like Vesuvius, steaming menacingly, the steam drifting slowly across the trenches like mustard gas.

The remains of the leaning shed of Pisa were still scattered across the garden. The deep trenches held his attention as though he had been drugged.

'What am I looking at?' he wondered. 'How on earth could this have happened; it's as though the place has been bombed. Look at those trenches and the shell-holes! Is it meant to be a model of a battlefield?'

The man was clearly bewildered. Horatio noticed his grandfather's face had fixed itself into a stare, his mouth open in a rictus of shock as he gave his own, rather full description of what had happened.

'What on earth is this grandson of mine on about?' he wondered. 'The man is mad! He doesn't need money to fix things, he needs treatment!'

The grandparents felt sorry for Gladys who was unable to get a word in edgeways. It was clear the stress had taken its toll on her: she just wanted a fag and a lie down.

Perhaps the final straw that convinced the grandparents to back out of the house quickly was Horatio's diatribe on the latest communist thinking followed by the rather badly timed statement, spoken clearly and with some conviction:

'I'm going to be a Wallaby next month.'

That did it! That he was certifiable was now clear. The best plan was to drive away and find a café somewhere where they could calm their nerves and have a cup of sweet restorative tea.

The Rover was a powerful car, which showed as it sped off in a cloud of smoke that it had never produced before, its accelerator being pushed to the floor for the very first time. The end of the street was reached in seconds and the car disappeared round the corner, never to return.

Gladys gazed at Horatio with a blank stare, mimicking the drooping ash on her Woodbine. She was unable to believe he'd just looked such a gift horse in the mouth, refusing a significant cash gift from his grandparents. She now realised she was destined to continue to live amongst Horatio's house-improvement schemes for many years.

A fresh Woodbine was lit and her asthma pump used on the 'high' setting.

***

Six months later, Lavender had found a nice house in the foothills of Llanelli, away from the railway sidings and the tinplate works. Arthur was reluctantly happy with his new surroundings: he'd not had to do a thing to get so nicely set up. He even began to feel a little soft on Lavender; she wasn't such a bad catch after all.

Also from Y Lolfa:

£3.95

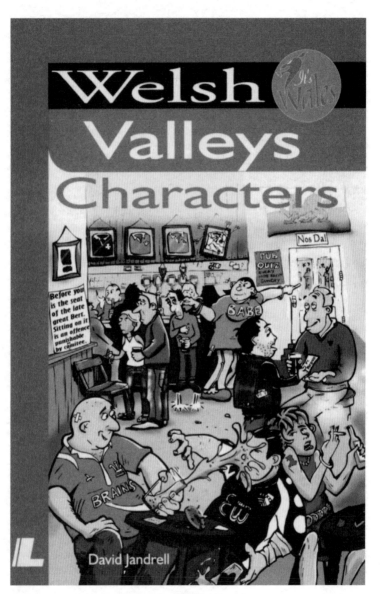

£3.95